"Rick Robinson's catalogue is filled with award-winning thrillers that demonstrate the keen intellect that has made the author a successful attorney and masterful political strategist. His latest offering, Alligator Alley, *however, is an immensely satisfying departure from political intrigue that distinguishes itself as a novel written straight from the heart.*

This is not to imply that Alligator Alley *is anything less than smartly written. To the contrary, the novel crackles with the dialogue readers have come to expect from Robinson and the plot has enough twists to satisfy every reader. Rather this novel stands out from Robinson's previous works as a very personal declaration for the author. Every line of* Alligator Alley *resonates with honesty as the author tells the story of a life not quite passed, blending sweet nostalgia, and the bitter tang of regret into a heady cocktail that everyone of a certain age has sampled. Some have savored. And a lucky few have hoisted to toast the adventures that still lay ahead.*

With Alligator Alley, *Robinson has achieved what every writer aspires to accomplish at least once in a career: He's written a life's work. In* Alligator Alley, *Robinson has created a very special novel that will not only satisfy current fans and certainly garner him still more well-deserved accolades, but will unquestionably stand the tests of time and earn a rightful place among other works that so poignantly and accurately capture the human condition. If* Huckleberry Finn *is the field book for boys eager to explore adolescence and* The Catcher in the Rye *is a manual for teens apprehensively approaching adulthood, then Robinson's* Alligator Alley *is the definitive (and destined to be classic) guide for all of those who have navigated the dire straits of adulthood but still quest for something more."*

—Eyre Price, Author

D1225381

Alligator Alley

Rick Robinson

Publisher Page
an imprint of Headline Books, Inc.
Terra Alta, WV

Alligator Alley

By Rick Robinson

copyright ©2013Rick Robinson

Publisher Page
P.O. Box 52
Terra Alta, WV 26764
www.PublisherPage.com
www.AuthorRickRobinson.com

Tel/Fax: 800-570-5951
Email: mybook@headlinebooks.com
www.HeadlineBooks.com

Publisher Page is an imprint of Headline Books, Inc.

ISBN 13 978-0-938467-65-6

Library of Congress Control Number: 2013935042

Robinson, Rick
        Alligator Alley / Rick Robinson
        p. cm.
        ISBN 978-0-938467-65-6
        1. Florida-fiction 2. Alligator Alley-fiction 3. Seminole-
        fiction

To Clifford "Chippie" Thompson

And to Bill and Tom Gaither who wanted to be him; to my sisters – Ruthie Staley and Claudia Singleton – to my cousins – Jim Wear, Dave Wear, Ken Houp, Gary Houp, Bob Bethel, Terry Bethel, and Cindy Schrode who knew and miss him; to Kevin Kelly who may be him and, last but certainly not least, to the long lost alligators of Prisoner's Lake.

Rudy and Chippie

"The case of the Seminoles constitutes at present the only exception to the successful efforts of the Government to remove the Indians to the homes assigned them west of the Mississippi River."

—President Martin Van Buren

"Let our last sleep be in the graves of our native land."

—Billy "Osceola" Powell

"Send my mail to the Rosarita Beach Café."

—Warren Zevon

Chapter One

If hitting fifty is the new forty, I'm not sure I want to stick around for sixty.

Up until today, I tried to update my Facebook status on a daily basis. But the last several days of my life have turned my entire world upside down. My life has been altered in ways I cannot even begin to explain via social networking in a status update. I am having trouble comprehending how my values have changed over the last week of my life – how my mind has expanded while, at the same time, my world-view has gotten smaller. A week following my celebration of a half century on this earth, a vicious battle of macro versus micro is being fought between my ears. To the victor goes my life.

Facebook. It would be absurd now to try to communicate my emotions with pictures and words on a smart phone screen. Yet, it was not all that long ago when I tried.

Last week, I was still part of the cyber world of social networking lemmings. While I sat on an airplane waiting to fly to southern Florida, I tapped a new "status" into my phone to send to 223 of my closest friends. It was an ominous choice of words for declaring the start of my fifty-first year on this earth. Although separated by distance from my cyber pals, I sighed to myself as I hit the send button on the phone and contemplated the responses I might get from those united in the bond of impersonal internet interaction.

At the time, I was amused by the irony of the status update I just posted. The words I sent into cyberspace might have a tongue-in-cheek tone to them, but they did not even begin to reflect the deep and growing melancholy affecting my soul. It had been growing for quite some time, but peaked that very day. The fact was, despite the overwhelming number of internet buddies I electronically befriended over the past several years, I was spending my fiftieth birthday traveling alone. The feeling was peaceful on one hand and alarming on the other.

The very fact I was sitting by myself did not specifically bother me. Ever since I was a kid, I have enjoyed being by myself. My great uncle taught me that being alone was okay. It gave me time to put my life in order. Being alone can give you perspective ... time to think ... peace of mind. But the actual reason I was alone on this trip was troubling. The quiet was eating at me. I was discovering that solitude could be both a blessing and a curse. Being alone with your thoughts is not pleasant when your thoughts are trending dark.

Snow blanketed the ground on either side of the runway and the smell of glycol filled the fuselage as they de-iced the chariot that would take me to warmer weather. The sky was a cold, cloudless blue and the ground a sea of white. My goal for Florida was to keep the blue skies, but to change out the white snow for white sand. I desperately needed the change of scenery. My life seemed as full of jarring contrasts as the change in weather I was about to experience.

Alone. My own personal choices had brought me to that point of singular isolation and I take full responsibility for picking one option over another. Still, there are a few days in my life for which I wish I could be given the mystic "do-over" – the wave of a metaphysical magic wand that would allow me to go back in time and change a choice made too hastily. Maybe a thoughtful zig here rather than a thoughtless zag there would have led to a suitable companion sitting in the seat next to me, instead of some grey-haired elderly widow babbling on about her winter condo in Bay Harbor.

I had not felt that kind of deep, soulful regret since the last time I visited my old college campus. Walking in and out of the buildings of your youth can bring back painfully happy memories. Thoughts of a passionate kiss in a stairwell had left me wondering as to what would have happened if I had take it further than a kiss. Where is she today? Is she happy? Or, like me, does she suffer similar, silent lament? For young people, everything is fresh and new on a college campus. Wide-eyed students wander from class-to-class, universal youthful cluelessness evident in their every movement. Visiting a college campus as an alumni reminds you of your age.

As I sat and contemplated my half-century milestone, I looked around at the happy families boarding the plane. Watching the choreography of chaotic movement forced a sardonic grin. Many of the mothers and fathers did not look much older than college students themselves. They were smiling and laughing. What choices had they made in their lives that somehow entitled them to smile? But smile they did as they struggled to shove their children's overstuffed Hello Kitty backpacks under the seats in front of them.

Maybe it was the backpack, I thought. Personally, as a DINK – Double Income, No Kids – I did not know that joy in my life. I was the first of three children from a hardworking, middle-class family from a small southern river town. I had divorced my first wife long before there was any dis-

11

cussion of continuing the family lineage – a decision that turned out well for both of us. She went "searching for herself" and ended up marrying a biker. Today they are running a bar out west somewhere. It was a good thing we never had kids. Deciding child custody and scheduling visitations probably would have revolved around Bike Week.

When I met Victoria, my current wife, she made it abundantly clear from the beginning of our relationship she was more interested in corporate advancement than having any children. At the time, I was of the same mindset and agreed. We were young and enjoyed the lifestyle of being unencumbered. There can be worse things in life than engaging in sex for pure pleasure rather than pro-creation.

Over the years, I watched as my friends became ostensibly burdened by the complicated drama and expense of children. I got more than my fill of kids from visiting my younger siblings on holidays and other family gatherings. Still, I was alone on my birthday because climbing the stairs leading to the glass ceiling was more important to my wife than being with me for a personal milestone. A big meeting caused her to cancel her ticket, insisting that I go alone and relax. I nearly asked the ticket agent at the airport if my wife had actually booked her seat in the first place, but remained silent. I am sure she did book her ticket. However, not knowing for sure better fit my mood of self-indulgent pity. I shifted uncomfortably in my seat with the realization I was perfectly content spending this day as a martyr nailed to the cross of life.

The laughter of one traveling family caught my attention – a mom and dad with a little girl who appeared to be about five years old. All three were talking, laughing, smiling – I shook my head and wondered if those smiles and laughter resulted from the jubilation of youth or the inherent ignorance of inexperience. The parents looked so damn young in their tight jeans and Sinatra-style hats. Obviously, they had not made enough bad decisions yet to reflect upon life with regret.

The pair was young and attractive. Both were wearing trendy clothes and sporting tattoos. He had a cross on his upper forearm; she a red heart on the side of her right breast. The tattoo on the young woman was sexy peeking out from her v-neck tee shirt. I tried to envision what it would look like in twenty-five years when she reached my age. In twenty or thirty years, tattoo removal shops will probably become as popular as tattoo parlors are today – store fronts where the middle-aged can go without embarrassment and pay someone to remove that "what the hell was I thinking" moment from their lives. I chuckled out loud at the thought. If only removal of emotional bad decisions were as easy as removing tattoos. Someone could open up a chain of regret removal parlors and make a fortune.

There's probably an internal life meter in which lament increases over time and regret becomes as natural as sleep. Get to the "red zone" on the gauge and the id calls in a prescription for an overdose of sleeping pills.

Was that what was bothering my soul – the long-term effect of short-term decisions on my personal happiness?

Maybe.

But, on the first day of my vacation, there was no immediate time for such reflection. The flight attendant tapped me on the shoulder and told me to shut down my electronic devices. Inner-monologue could wait for another day. Our wings were fully de-iced and my flight to Miami was third in line for takeoff.

I hit the "flight mode" button on the new iPhone my wife gave me, in absentia, as a birthday present, knowing my upbeat, snarky, online persona was zipping to the netherworld of Facebook. In science fiction, Philip Dick asked if androids dream of electric sheep. I wondered at how our artificial social media selves continue their apparent cheerful wakefulness even when we (and our devices) sleep.

At the start of my venture into middle age, I find I am reduced to communicating the great indifference I have to life via Facebook status updates. Regrettably, my health insurance plan sucks and does not include any meaningful mental health coverage. So, Facebook, for me, is a substitute for psychiatric counseling sessions. At least in social media, I am in "in network."

Facebook ... damn. I cannot remember the exact point in time when I became a cyber-geek. Believe me, I have tried. And, each time I conduct that mental exercise, I cannot pinpoint a particular day when my life became as sad as a nerd dressed in a Jedi Knight robe, waiting in line for the premiere of the latest Star Wars movie. Oh, the parameters of the time line are pretty clear. One day in 1987, I was attending a computer training course, and I had to ask where the "ON" button was located on the complex "adding-machine" in front of me. Today, I have an iPhone, three desktop computers, one lap top and countless thumb drives.

When I was in my thirties, I spent most of my free time in bars. Now, I seem to spend most of my free time clicking back and forth between Facebook, LinkedIn, MySpace, Twitter and checking for messages in my four separate email accounts.

On the left side of the time line of my life, I was cool. I wore black tennis shoes, listened to REM and ate at restaurants where people needed actual reservations to be seated. Today, with my spot on the line pushing further each day to the right, I listen to talk radio and eat at Outback (but only if it is one of their free wifi locations). I still wear the black tennis shoes, but do so only for the arch support. REM broke up and Michael Stipes looks as old as me.

In college, I smoked pot and popped speed. I still have a drug problem, but my pills are chosen by my family physician – Lipitor, Flomax and Zoloft.

I see the startling differences, yet I just cannot figure out when I actually changed. Maybe I should rummage through the box on the closet shelf looking for the bottle that once held the first psychotropic I ever purchased legally. Maybe that was the day I started to change.

And it's not just the gadgets and the meds. I have noticed myself using language that screams out "geek." At times, the word "kids" flows into the air when I am referring to kids, uhh … people, in their thirties. I refer to the music I purchase for my iPhone as records. Jesus, I am one good utterance of "twenty-three skidoo" away from being my old man. Twenty-three skidoo – I even fuck that up and think of it in terms of an era gone by rather than youthful code for smoking pot.

It is not that becoming my old man would be such a bad thing. My dad was a great person whom I loved and admired. But starting a second half century in life is a milestone I never really thought about until it arrived. I cannot say that I am happy about it.

Look at me. I tweet for Christ's sake. When was it that my life became so important that I sought to share it with strangers in 127 characters or less? Do people really want to know when I am headed to the gym for a hard workout? God, I hope not. That would make them as screwed up as me, maybe more so.

Perhaps joining the cyber-age was my way of trying to convince myself that I was still young and had already led a successful life. As expected by my parents, teachers, spouses and former self, I have done okay and over the past several years have been quick with a key-stroke to let everyone know it. Then again, maybe, my incessant computer use has just been a way for me to convince myself that I am not a loser. I have led a life in which I have been more afraid of success than failure. When you wrap yourself in the charade of success, you live with a fear that someone will peek behind the curtain and discover it's all been a sham. Failure is real. Success is smoke and mirrors.

Success and failure both have the same mental foundation for me. I revel in the fact that I grew up in a small town in Kentucky. I feel sorry for people my age who grew up in big cities, and pity the kids today who grow up in sterile subdivisions where their youthful memories will consist almost entirely of their moms driving them to soccer practice in a cul-de-sac based minivan. As a kid, the members of my family considered themselves to be living in the South, but we were a fifteen-cent bus ride across a bridge spanning the Ohio River from a northern manufacturing center. The contrast had its benefits. I lived in a small town, but I had some of the accompaniment of a big town – sports, plays, movies, that kind of stuff.

Because Kentucky was a neutral state in the War of Northern Aggression, many people in the Deep South do not consider the Commonwealth to be truly "southern." Most Kentuckians would argue the proposition, my parents being of that viewpoint. Grandma, in particular, insisted that we were southern and would argue her heritage with her friends who lived across the river in Ohio. In testament to our rebel lineage, Grandma taught my mom how to make city chicken and hot slaw, a southern meal the appreciation for which is lost on refined Yankee palates.

For those too young to remember (read – the kids), city chicken was what the local butcher created by sticking a wooden skewer through the throw away cuts of pork he prepared for his high-payin' customers. It was kind of a poor man's tofu, with heavy breading and extra fat. Mom would roll the skewers in cracker crumbs and fry them in an iron skillet with what seemed to have an inch of bacon grease in it.

After the pig-on-a-stick was cooked to perfection, Mom added sugar and vinegar to a portion of the bacon grease, which she then poured over diced cabbage she had grown in the garden. Crumple the bacon on top of it and – *voila* – hot slaw.

My dad claimed he could actually hear his aorta slam shut as we ate this delicacy. The combination of city chicken and hot slaw was outlawed by the Department of Health and Human Services in 1999 – or at least it should have been.

My small town rearing was the foundation of all that I, for either better or worse, had become. Larger than life characters with grand nicknames like Stinker, Stumpy, Lightning, and Ducky roamed our streets. Nicknames are one thing about small towns which make those who live there unique. Everyone has a nickname and wears it like a badge of honor, even Stinker.

Some nicknames in small towns are by birthright. Where I grew up, entire families had the same nicknames that covered several generations. One of my best friends growing up was Ducky. Ducky's Dad was Ducky and he had three brothers called Ducky. Their boys – all Duckies. My friend Ducky moved away after college. I called his office one day and asked his secretary if "Ducky" was around. She told him that someone from his hometown was on the phone.

In the world of nicknames, my dad was known as "Angel." My grandmother thought her son got his nickname because he was a good boy who stayed out of trouble. The truth was, he got the nickname because he looked like a 50s era big-time wrestler on television by the same name. Dad was the Angel. Thus, to all his friends, so was I. A few of Angel's friends called me Cupid, but the subtlety of the name was lost on most of his pals.

Others in our town earned their name, sometimes via some unspeakable carnage, horrible incident in life or personal flaw. There was one woman in particular, Mrs. Morris, who had a knack for giving nicknames that had a nasty bite to them. When she gave out a nickname, it stuck. Lightning had been hit by lightning as a kid. If Stumpy had been one inch shorter or ten pounds heavier, he would have been totally round. Baldy had ringworms in the third grade and the doctor shaved his head. And Stinker, well, that goes without saying.

Mrs. Morris lived two doors down from a family who all had peculiar looks. The oldest son she nicknamed Ugly and his sister Double-Ugly. In a small town, you do not mess with the person in charge of bestowing nicknames.

I drove through my old hometown a day or two before my trip. In many respects it looked the same as when I had been a kid. A couple of years ago, they filmed a movie in our downtown. The setting for the movie was Yonkers, New York in the summer of 1942. It was perfect. My hometown still looks more like Yonkers in 1942 than Yonkers does today.

But I digress – back to last week's plane flight.

Before following the orders of my flight attendant to turn

off my personal electronic devices, I looked at my Facebook profile page – James Conrad, 50 on the dot, married, no kids, college educated, bank vice president, who likes to read nonfiction and watch sports … blah, blah, blah.

Birthday wishes filled my Facebook wall posts.

Then I saw it – my profile picture. Even on a small iPhone screen, it stood out to me. I was old; I could deal with that issue. But the crow's feet on my eyes and the wrinkles on my forehead gave me a withered. lost look – unfulfilled. I ran my fingers across the top of my skull and realized that gray hair felt coarser than the brown bangs of my youth.

Youth. When I was a kid, my mom always prepared my favorite meal in celebration that another year had passed – city chicken and hot slaw, of course. Dessert was a home-made cake with sweet vanilla icing. My mouth watered like Pavlov's dog's. I grabbed a granola bar from my computer bag and ripped open the wrapper.

"Happy fucking birthday indeed."

"Electronic devices off, seatbacks forward and tray tables locked in their upright position. We're ready for take-off."

I closed my eyes hoping that sleep was a cure for middle-age melancholy.

*   *   *

The young boy sat in the bed of the orange 1965 Ford F-100 pickup. An old man, his mother's uncle, drove. His father sat in the passenger seat with his right arm hanging out the window. The boy bounced around, up and down, on the colorful Indian blanket his uncle placed on the bed of the truck for him to sit upon. The old man's dog steadied himself on one side, hanging his head over the rear quarter panel.

Fishing gear – assorted rods, reels and tackle boxes – rattled against the side of the truck bed. Three yellow mesh bags, labeled Indian River Citrus, were wedged against the truck's back gate.

It was Saturday afternoon and the small downtown was abuzz with weekend activity. As the truck made its way up Elm Street, the boy looked from side-to-side at the mix of people wandering the sidewalks. Women in plain, conservative dresses looked in shop windows. Men with broad smiles and madras-plaid shirts shook the hands of other men and slapped each other on the back. A marquee stuck out from the movie theater announcing that *The Last Tango in Paris* starring Marlon Brando was playing for an extra week.

A large man with slicked back, black hair wearing a stained white apron stood in front of a store front diner smoking a cigarette. A red neon sign proclaiming "PETE's" flickered in the window.

The boy patted his hands on his legs and the dog cautiously walked across the bed before lying down in the boy's lap. He rubbed the dog behind the ears.

"You okay back there, boy?" The driver hollered as he pulled up to a red light.

"Yes, sir," the boy shouted in reply. The truck started up again and the wind flowed through his sandy brown crew cut. He heard the old man laugh as they rolled down the street. Everybody loved the old man's laugh. It was loud and full of life.

Albert Clarke was the old man's name, but everyone in town knew him as "Gator" – a nickname he acquired from his yearly winter hunting and fishing trips to the Florida Everglades. He was thin and tall, but he had strong muscular arms. His gray hair seemed to flow naturally in multiple directions at one time and still not seem unkempt. He wore thick, black horn-rimmed glasses. Unlike everyone else on the town's street, Gator always had a deep tan on his long face. Even in the winter, his skin was golden brown. His laugh was his trademark. "If you're going to take the time and effort to laugh," he once told the boy, "make sure you laugh loud enough for everyone to hear ya."

The truck came to a quick stop when Gator spied a car leaving a parking place and he threw on the brakes. The boy and the dog both worked to steady themselves against the jerky movements of the truck. The dog walked to the side of the truck bed as if observing his master's parking job. When the truck was parked, the kid jumped from the bed and joined the two older men on the sidewalk. Gator pointed at the dog. "Wait here, Hadjo," he said. "I'll bring ya some water in a minute." As if he had understood every word, the mutt went over to the thick Indian blanket and lay down. The other man, the boy's father, put a nickel in the parking meter next to the truck and led the way down the street. Cars honked their horns and Gator waved in reply.

The trio walked to the store front of a dry goods shop and looked in the window. The older man pointed to a pair of light blue, high-top tennis shoes sitting next to a red, white and blue American Basketball Association basketball. "Them the ones ya want?" he asked the boy.

"Yes, sir," he replied excitedly, nearly pressing his nose against the window to get a good look.

"Then let's go get us a pair," Gator nodded and winked.

The ring of a hand bell tied onto the door with twine announced the trio's entrance to Maley's Dry Goods. Four aisles led from front to back with shelves displaying everything from clothes to toys. Maley's was the place in town where you could buy just about anything you needed, except food. Children's shoes were against the outside wall of the first aisle. The widow Maley, a large, round-faced woman with saggy upper arms, stood behind the cash register.

"Hello, Gator," greeted Mrs. Maley. "I heard you were back in town." She smiled at him and waved towards the other man. "Afternoon, Angel."

"Howdy, Margaret," Gator replied, winking at her when no one else was watching. Margaret blushed and looked away.

"Margaret," said Angel, nodding his head in recognition of the store's owner as he headed to the aisle displaying socks and underwear.

"Wrestle any alligators this year?" Margaret asked with a mild hint of sarcasm in her scratchy voice.

"Only the ones in my dreams," Gator smiled. He raised his index finger for emphasis. "They don't chomp back as much."

Margaret laughed at his joke. Everybody always seemed to laugh at Gator's jokes.

"Margaret?" Gator asked, lowering an eyebrow in her direction. "Are you still carryin' a torch for me?"

"Oh, Gator," Margaret blushed. "I see you're still as ornery as ever."

"You bet ya," Gator smiled. He loved to flirt with all the ladies in town, especially the widows.

"What brings you here today?" she asked, pointing to the sporting goods in the rear of the store. "I got some new bass lures for you to look at back by the fishin' poles. And there are some fresh night crawlers in the Frigidaire."

"Not here for me," Gator informed Margaret.

"Oh," she replied with interest.

"Here today for the boy," said Gator. He pulled the youngster to his side and proudly pushed him front and center. "I was in Florida when he turned ten last month and I flat out missed his birthday. I need to make up for it by gettin' him some of them new fancy gym shoes."

"Adidas Americanas," the boy blurted out in excitement. "The royal blue low cuts, just like Dan Issel wears."

"Manners," instructed Angel sternly. The boy had broken a cardinal rule of the family by speaking before he had actually been spoken to.

The boy lowered his head and blushed. "Sorry, Daddy … Uncle Al, Mrs. Maley."

Mrs. Maley smiled her approval of Angel's verbal rebuff. Gator's opposite reaction showed in his frown and wrinkled brow.

"The boy wants them shoes the Kentucky Colonels wear, Margaret," Gator interjected. "Don't know who Dan Issel is, but let's get him a pair."

"Gladly," said Margaret as she pulled the old wooden foot measure off the wall. "Come over here, Jimmy, and let's see what size you're wearing these days."

"And when we're done," Gator instructed, "go out in the truck and get you some Florida oranges and grapefruit. Hadjo's out there guarding them for ya."

"Oh, Gator, you spoil me."

"Straight from the Indian River, my dear Margaret," he smiled at the old woman and winked. "Only the best for you."

Chapter Two

With new gym shoes proudly peeking out from underneath the rolled-up hems of his cousin's hand-me-down Levis, Jimmy Conrad followed his father and great uncle up the street to Duke's Rock Bar. There were several bars on the main drag of downtown and a dozen or more scattered around the city, but the Rock Bar was the center of the most serious drinking activity. As the trio walked up the street, Jimmy kept quiet in anticipation of seeing the inside of a real bar for the first time as a patron.

Jimmy looked up and down the main drag, hoping one of his chums would spy him entering the Rock Bar. No one he knew had ever been inside a bar before to actually sit down and have a soft drink and he wanted bragging rights. All his friends had ponied up to the soda counter at Pete's for a phosphate or a malt, but none had partaken inside the dens of iniquity that were normally reserved for adults. A witness to this historic first could verify his adventure and make him a hero to those in his age bracket. Unfortunately, while the sidewalks were busy with activity, none of his friends were anywhere within sight. Still, the lack of a pair of verifying eyes did not dampen his spirit.

"Remember now," instructed Angel as they approached the door. "Whatever you do, don't tell your mother that I let you come in with me and her uncle to visit with Duke."

"Don't worry, Daddy," Jimmy replied, scratching his temple in an uncomfortable movement, showing his unease at the thought of lying to his mother. "I'll tell her I sat out in the truck with Hadjo, just like you said. I won't tell her you took me inside."

"Aw, bull," mumbled Gator, kicking up some imaginary dust from the sidewalk with his foot. "It's just a damn bar. You tell that niece of mine that the boy ain't goin' to hell just because he had a soda in a bar."

"I'll let you tell her that," Angel replied, nodding at Jimmy to confirm their family conspiracy. "We're perfectly fine with telling her a lie to keep both of us out of Dutch. Right?"

Jimmy nodded his head in silent affirmation. If it was good enough for his dad, it was good enough for him.

Gator was having none of Angel's logic. "A bar's one of the few places in life where a man can feel himself," he snapped as they crossed the street. He put his arm around Jimmy's small shoulder as they walked and Gator looked down at him. "Ain't nobody puttin' on airs in a good bar. All the town drunks and God-fearin' Christians are the same behind them doors," Gator said, pointing at the entrance. "A good bar is a good bar. If ya ever go into a bar and ya feel uneasy, you're probably in the wrong bar. Got that?"

"Yes, sir," Jimmy replied. He had no earthly idea what his great uncle had just told him, but he was not about to admit it. He simply stored the advice in his young mind with all the other simple rules of life that Gator was prone to give him.

"Someday you'll find yourself in a bar, Jimmy," Gator continued. "And ya may not know if it's a good place to be or a bad place to be. In that situation, you gotta know how to act. Otherwise, folks will take advantage of ya."

"Yes, sir," Jimmy replied confidently, yet still totally confused.

"Maybe," Angel interjected as they reached the bar and he opened the door to the establishment. "But if his momma finds out we took Jimmy in here today, we're both liable to be meetin' our Maker before our time."

Jimmy walked into the bar in silent awe. Long shadows quickly shot across the floor of Duke's Rock Bar, as the open door allowed the outside light to invade the room's thick, smoky confines. The boy's attention darted around as his eyes adjusted to the darkness. There were windows, but they had been painted gray and allowed little, if any, natural light into the room. The glass domes that covered the lights on the ceiling were yellow from cigarette smoke. Three men sat at the bar, still wearing their railroad coveralls from working the night shift at the Southern engine house. Another group of men sat silently at a table in the corner playing cards, a small pile of coins in the center of the table. The wood floor smelled old and oily. There was so much to take in that Jimmy was quickly overwhelmed. His senses were overloaded.

"Well, well, look who's back up North," shouted the bartender. "Hey, boys, the prodigal son has returned." Everybody liked Duke Bodkin. He was a big, bald-headed man, who from his spot behind the tap of the town's favorite watering hole, gave out more news than could ever be reported in the weekly newspaper. "The Crown Prince of the Florida Everglades is home. When did ya get back, Gator?" Duke reached across the mahogany bar laid on top of concrete and rocks and shook Gator's hand enthusiastically.

"Wednesday, I think," Gator replied, returning the shake with equal gusto. "I forgot how fast news travels around here. How's business, Duke?"

"News travelin' fast? Around here?" Duke replied mockingly. "You gotta' be kidding. Tell-a-gram, tell-a-graph or tell one of the people in this town." As he was often prone to do, Duke laughed loudly at his own joke. "Business is good. Economy is slow, but people are still drinkin'."

Gator looked up at the stuffed alligator head hanging on the wall over the bottles of liquor. "Still got 'Big John' up there I see," Gator said. "He put up one helluva fight."

"Yup," replied Duke. "And I'm still tellin' everyone who walks in here the story about how you caught him down in the swamp with that Injun' boy you're always talking about."

As the men talked, Jimmy was still busy taking it all in. The wall behind the bar had a mural painted on it of a river and its shoreline. The painting was probably once a vibrant green, but it had lost its luster from years of being exposed to nicotine and smoke. Packs of Bromo Seltzer hung on a rack behind the bar, right next to the St. Joseph aspirin, each 10 cents a dose. A Burger Beer sign advertised WCPO King of TV Bowling. There was a sign on the cash register: "CREDIT makes enemies. Let's be friends." Jimmy was not exactly sure what it meant, but he found it funny nevertheless.

Duke looked at the boy's father. "Howdy, Angel."

"Howdy back at you, Duke," Angel replied. "How's the family?"

"They're all good, pal." Duke's grin spread across his face as he looked down at the boy. "And, speaking of family, who's that ya got with you today?"

"Duke, you remember my boy, Jimmy, don't you?" Angel asked as he reached down, picked up Jimmy and plopped him down onto a barstool.

"Oh, that can't be 'Little Angel' Jimmy Conrad," Duke said, throwing his hands in the air in mock surprise. "He couldn't be that grown up? Boy, did you drive up here?"

"No, sir," Jimmy replied, his cheeks blushing red. "I'm not old enough yet."

"Could have fooled me," Duke replied. "You look old enough to drive. We aren't going to be callin' him Little Angel much longer. You'll be taller than your old man in a couple of years." Duke looked over at Angel. "And thank God he's not wearin' his hair long. All those kids growing their hair long is making me sick."

The boy averted his eyes to his new gym shoes and smiled a large, shy grin. Secretly, he wanted to let his crew cut grow out a bit, but was afraid to ask his parents for permission to do so. Despite the comment, the boy liked Duke. He tossed baseball all the time with Duke's son, Steve. An errant throw one day had caused a broken basement window. He was happy that Steve's dad had remembered him by name and yet did not bring up the window mishap. "I've got an extra Gary Nolan baseball card today," Jimmy said as he reached into his pocket and pulled out the cards. He handed the card of the Cincinnati Reds' pitcher to Duke. "I got it in a pack Uncle Albert brought me from Florida. Could you give it to Steve, please? He probably needs it to complete series two." Maybe a bribe would keep Duke from mentioning the broken window to Angel.

"Yes, sir, I certainly will," he replied with a smile and a wink. He looked at the card before stuffing it into his shirt pocket. "What's everyone want?"

"Give Angel a draft and I'll take a rock and rye," said Gator, reaching in his pocket for his wallet. "And after the boy takes some water out to the truck for Hadjo, give Jimmy here a Royal Crown and a deviled ham sammich on white bread."

"Thanks, Uncle Albert," Jimmy replied. Duke filled up two paper cups with water and pushed them across the bar. "I'll take the water out to Hadjo. Me and him are buddies."

"Is John R. in the back?" Gator laid a five-dollar bill on the bar to pay the tab and shuffled through his wallet to count his remaining money. "I need to get a bet down on the daily double at Latonia. I got a hot tip from a groom I know out there."

"Al," said Angel, nodding his head towards Jimmy.

"Damn it, Angel," Gator shook his head in a non-apologetic fashion. "It ain't gonna kill the boy to know I drink and bet on the horses, too. I even smoked a cigarette once or twice in my life."

"Come on, Al." Angel had a degree of frustration in his voice. Gator had his own ways and let everyone in the family know it. He was not ashamed to speak his mind. Still, Gator's frank nature in front of his son was at times frustrating to Angel. He knew Jimmy was going to learn about the vices of men someday, but he would rather it happen in its own due time. "Son, why don't you go on out and take care of Hadjo," Angel instructed, pointing to the door. "I need to talk to your uncle."

Jimmy took the water out to the pickup truck. Hadjo stood up and wagged his tail as Jimmy found his pan and poured in the water. As Hadjo drank, Jimmy rubbed the old dog behind the ear. "You got a great life, old boy," Jimmy said. "You get to go around with Uncle Al all the time and go fishin' whenever you want and live off the land. Someday when I get old, I'm gonna be just like you guys and go from place to place, working for awhile and then moving on to fish for awhile. And, I'll have a good old dog just like you." He leaned forward and whispered into the dog's ear, "And we'll go to bars together, drinkin' and gamblin' too."

*   *   *

"What you need, mon?" asked Everton Santiago, the handsome Jamaican bartender at the pool bar of the exclusive Ocean Reef Club in Key Largo.

"Anything with dark rum in it," I replied as I flopped onto a barstool. "Surprise me." I fumbled for my cigarettes and found my lighter in my pocket. "And I need an ashtray."

"You got it, mon," Everton said as he grabbed a bottle and poured a heavy-handed shot of Myers rum into a plastic cup. A splash of pineapple juice followed. Everton's beaming smile made him look younger than his graying hair indicated. "There you go, mon," he said. Everton had the kind of voice and delivery where everything he said seemed to end in a laugh.

The Ocean Reef Club is a private residential community on the north tip of Key Largo. The club at the community's hotel is the town's central gathering point. Custom-made golf carts and expensive cars fill the parking lot. It was evident that Everton knew all the regulars by name and quickly got to know the visiting snowbirds like myself who flew south to expatriate America without leaving its actual borders. If the bar was the central meeting place of the town, Everton Santiago was evidently the island's mayor. His heavy island accent indicated that he was a long way from his home in Hopewell, Jamaica.

As he put my drink in front of me, he asked, "You just get here, my friend?"

"Last night," I replied, as I lit up my first cigarette of the afternoon and drew in a deep breath. I have been telling myself to quit smoking for months. I even tried the nicotine gum. It gave me hiccups. Today with my first drink already in hand, it sure tasted good. "I flew into Miami yesterday morning."

"I didn't see you around here yesterday," Everton said. He spoke with a quiet authority that indicated he was the kind of bartender who knew everyone on the island and everything they were doing. I made a mental note.

"It was a nice day, so I hung around at the dog track for a couple of hours," I said as I nodded towards the hotel. "I checked in here after dinner, then slept in through breakfast."

"Very good, mon." He slapped a towel on the bar and cleaned some water off the surface. "You do any good at the track?"

"I got lucky and hit a trifecta," I replied, smiling. I rubbed my fingers together. "I came out a couple of hundred ahead."

"I don't like the dogs or jai alai," Everton replied. He paused, smiled and spoke slowly. "But I love to go up to the casino on the reservation and play Caribbean Poker, mon."

"Too exotic for me," I laughed. "You've got to think too much."

"So, did you come down for the party last night?"

"I came down and had a night cap," I replied. The smoke rolled out of my mouth as I spoke. "It looked like there was a lot happening, but I didn't stay up too late. I was pretty tired from the trip. I had a couple of drinks and was ready for some sleep."

"Vacation?" Everton asked. His friendly nature made the conversation feel comfortable and inviting.

"Kind of," I replied as I took the first sip of my drink, smiling in appreciation of the stiff pour. "Yesterday was my fiftieth birthday. The trip is a present."

"Well, Happy Birthday, my new friend," he said with a sincerity in his voice I somehow believed.

"Thanks," I replied. "I'm looking forward to some serious relaxation this week."

"Well, this is the place to relax," said Everton. "Everyone thinks 'mañana' in the Keys."

Mañana – the time yet to come. "Yeah, I could use a little of that," I said. The drink was going down far too easily.

"Then you should come down tonight for the party," Everton instructed.

"Another party?" I asked. I had not planned on doing much partying, but I wanted to keep the conversation going.

"Yeah, mon," Everton exclaimed as he used the same towel he had used on the bar to wipe sweat from his brow. "Every night there is a big party here. Everyone on the island comes here for the action." He leaned in. "Lots of pretty ladies looking for fun."

I held up my left hand, exposing my wedding ring. "I'm allergic to fun."

"The ring doesn't matter to the ladies here," Everton replied. "For some of them, you're a safe night out."

"Safe night out?" I asked.

"Yes, sir," said Everton. "You're married. In their minds, you probably have as much to lose as they do."

"Thanks for the advice," I replied, shaking my head negatively at the suggestion of a romantic hook up. "I'm just here to have a few drinks, maybe do a little fishing and catch up on a lot of lost relaxation."

"Very well then, I'll take care of the drinks for you," he nodded. "You can take that part of your trip off your mind." He paused and looked like he was going through a mental rolodex of information. "And I can tell you some good places to go fishing, too."

I scooted my chair back and let the late morning sun hit my face. It seemed I had not seen the sun in months. Before taking off, I had been experiencing a bad case of seasonal depression that my daily dose of serotonin enhancers just could not cure. It was nice to start a personal relationship with the sun again. Blue sky and UV rays seemed to be what I needed. It was more than the warmth. It felt like the sun was literally soaking into my skin and into my bloodstream. I was starting to feel better with each sip of rum and pineapple juice.

I leaned forward, put my cigarette out, and grabbed the *Miami Herald* lying on the bar. I tried to concentrate on a front-page story about the death of a man at the nearby Seminole casino, but the briny smell of the salt air won the battle for my brain. I put the newspaper down on the bar and looked out towards the Atlantic. The crowded rows of pool umbrellas nearly blocked the view. I did not need the view to comfort me. I closed my eyes and let the warm sun, along with the sound of waves splashing against the shore, assure my brain that the Atlantic Ocean was only steps away. I had been at this bar for only a few minutes, but it suddenly seemed like a lifetime since I had last been anywhere else.

My eyes were forced open by the sounds of a man in a blue and yellow Hawaiian print shirt tuning an expensive red Stratocaster on a small covered stage right next to the bar. I looked over to the man. A sign behind the tip jar said "The Cool Island Sounds of Phil Tatro." We made eye contact.

"Nice ax," I said, nodding at the Strat. "It must be a bitch to keep it tuned in this humidity."

"Yeah." Tatro smiled in appreciation of the compliment. "You play?" he responded.

"A little acoustic," I said, then grinned. "Very little."

"Ever try an electric?" he laughed in response.

"I tried to be Slash in another life," I replied. "I quickly realized that I was an acoustic kind of guy." I pointed to my grey temples. "Quite honestly, I never had the hair for it."

Tatro laughed out loud at the reference. "Want to hear anything?" he asked while continuing to tune the Strat.

I paused for a minute. "Your favorite song," I replied.

Tatro obviously appreciated a request for anything other than another Jimmy Buffett song and started his set with a bluesy rendition of John Hiatt's *Buffalo River Home*. The sound of palm trees swaying to the ocean breeze offered a soothing rhythm as he sang.

"Pretty interesting story there." Everton tapped at the newspaper on the bar, snapping my attention away from the guitar player.

"What?" I had been busy getting lost in the song. "Which story?"

"That story you were reading in the newspaper," Everton replied, pointing at the headline.

"Oh, yeah," I said. "Some guy from Homestead died at the Seminole casino last month. It sounds like everybody's pretty fired-up about it. How'd he die?"

Everton raised his fluffy eyebrows and shook his head. "That's why everyone is mad. No one is really sure, mon."

"What do you mean," I asked, "no one is sure?"

"Before the family could get there to claim the man's body," Everton said, "the Seminole doctor on the reservation had already done an autopsy. He declared the man died of a heart attack and had his body cremated. When the family showed up, he was just a pile of ashes." Everton picked up my ashtray and dumped it out in the garbage for dramatic emphasis.

Everton suddenly had my attention with the bizarre story. I looked down at the paper as he put the ashtray back on the bar. "No shit?" I asked. "How can they do that?"

"Something about tribal law," Everton said as he nodded at a waiter walking past the bar. "The casino is on a Seminole reservation. Their law applies over the laws of our government. They cremated the dude and there's nothing the family can do about it."

I picked up the paper. As I started to read the story more closely, I noticed my drink was gone. "Another one," I said to Everton as I pushed the empty glass forward.

"You got it, mon," he replied.

Tribe Fights Release of Records

A Florida couple continues their fight in an effort to obtain records about the death of their son, Ramon Sanchez, at an Indian owned casino.

Last year, Sanchez and two friends went to the casino for a night of poker. Late in the evening, Sanchez collapsed at the table and died. Rather than calling county authorities, the death was investigated by the reservation based tribal coroner, Dr. Scott Yanah. Following an autopsy, the reservation cremated Sanchez's body. While the tribe released a death certificate indicating that Sanchez had died of a heart attack, they have continued to fight the release of any additional records about the death.

The efforts of the Sanchez family in attempting to recover the records have been hampered by the fact that the tribe has sovereign immunity, a legal doctrine that shields the tribe from laws that are not its own.

I looked up from the paper, not needing to read anything more to understand Everton's outrage. "Damn." I said. "That's harsh."

"You bet it is, mon," Everton nodded handing me a fresh drink. "If it happens on the reservation, the Seminole decide what happens. They do what they want up there."

I savored a sip of my fresh drink. While the story in the newspaper was intriguing to me, reading it caused my thoughts to wander. As a kid, I had visited my Uncle Al on a Seminole Indian reservation in the Everglades. The memory caused me to smile.

My Great Uncle Al Clarke had been labeled both a legend and a louse around my hometown. His whole life had revolved around hunting and fishing. He was a skilled carpenter. Yet, even during the Depression, if a job arose when the crappie were running at Lake Herrington, he would choose fishing over steady employment. He could play any musical instrument with strings and taught me the first chords I ever learned on guitar.

I loved the old man, followed at his boot heels and dreamed of growing up in his image. As an adult, a week didn't go by when I did not think about him ... his coke-bottle thick glasses ... the safari style helmet he wore when he was fishing ... the orderly way he arranged his fishing lures in his tackle box.

I grew up in a house way too small for the number of people sleeping there. I did not have my own room. None of us kids did. Only Mom and Dad had that convenience. As a child, I slept on an old Army cot in the same room with my grandma – Al's sister. A bureau, a dresser, a single bed, Grandma's sewing machine and I were all squeezed into a tiny room that overlooked a neighbor's beautiful rose garden.

I kept my most prized possessions—my baseball cards and G.I Joe—in a cardboard box under the cot. Grandma also let me tape three pictures above my pillow—an autograph from Dan Issel, a picture clipped from a Cincinnati Reds scorecard of Wayne Simpson, and a newspaper photograph of my uncle. In the newspaper photo, Uncle Al was holding down an alligator with a knee on its back. "Gators on a Spree," read the title of the photo.

Albert ('Gator) Clarke, who commutes between here and his winter home in the Florida Everglades, was the innocent, indirect cause of quite a stir in Devou Park on Tuesday night. His pet hobby – a dangerous one – is hunting alligator and wild boar. He has bagged a number of 'gators, some measuring 16 feet in length. Two of his favorite "baby" alligators, which he recently presented to Bobby McCabe, Devou Park superintendent, to be placed in the park's Behringer Museum, were the cause of the excitement Tuesday night. The 'gators escaped from their tank at the museum and made their way to Prisoner's Lake, frightening golfers and concert fans in their path. Mr. Clarke and the two "scare babies" are shown above, along with the stuffed head of one of the larger alligators he has bagged on his hunting trips.

The great alligator hunt made Uncle Al a legend to the men around our town. What he did to his wife was what made him a louse to all the women. Al, his best fishing buddy, Rudy, and two other men had a boat dock down on Lake Herrington where they would fish, drink, smoke cigars, and play pinochle. They called it Chimney Rock Boat Dock. It was where they spent most of their free time.

The four fishermen of Chimney Rock Boat Dock were very tight with their angling secrets. One time they told others at a local bar they soaked their lures in pickle juice to attract bass. The next day, boats cruised Lake Herrington with bottles of pickle juice filled with spoon-lures and spinners. The men were as clandestine with their fishing tips as the Masons are with their fraternal secrets.

Karma, however, caught up with them one day. In order to fish late into the evening, the men built a fire in a wash-bucket on the wood dock. A coal from the fire popped out and inadvertently set part of the dock on fire. The dock burned down to the waterline and took two wood johnboats and a canoe with it. When Uncle Al swore to rebuild the deck, his wife, my mom's aunt, laid down the law, and told him he had to choose between her and the fish. The fish won. He left.

The very same night my aunt delivered her ultimatum, Uncle Al tossed his fishing gear into his pickup truck and headed off for Florida. My aunt's heart was not the only one broken. I was devastated. I cried for days at the thought he was gone. My mom comforted me by telling me he would come home occasionally. At first that held up, and Uncle Al would come back once or twice a year to visit. Eventually, though, he quit coming back at all. My great uncle spent the twilight of his life living on a houseboat docked at an Indian tourist stop in the Florida Everglades.

"A Seminole Indian reservation," I mumbled.

"What?" Everton asked as he placed yet another drink in front of me.

"Nothing," I shook my head, slightly embarrassed that I had actually spoken the words out loud. "Thanks." I picked up the drink and stared out at the mangrove trees lining the inlet to the south of the bar.

As a boy, much to my mother's chagrin, I had idolized her uncle. At the time, I didn't understand what a divorce was and could not comprehend my mom's embarrassment at her uncle's change in marital status. It bothered her that I wanted to be like the old man, spending my days shirking responsibility in favor of fishing and hunting. The fact that a woman, a squaw, and her son lived with him on the houseboat was dealt with in polite conversation in hushed tones. Whenever I approached such family conversations, everyone stopped speaking. The silence was usually followed by someone saying "little pitchers have big ears." I still do not know what the fuck that means.

When my uncle was dying of cancer, we took a family vacation to Florida and visited with him for a day on the reservation. He played mandolin for me and gave me his favorite rod and reel and an old Gibson guitar. "To remember me by," he said. For some inexplicable reason, I had brought both of them with me on this trip.

The combination of the Atlantic's lapping rhythmic beat with the guitar player's song reminded me of how much unlike my uncle I had become. My malaise suddenly reappeared like the grim reaper.

"Hey, Everton," I said.

"Yeah, mon?"

"How long does it take to get from here to Alligator Alley?"

Chapter Three

I pulled myself begrudgingly out of the pool and staggered slowly over to the lounge chair I set up facing the ocean. Everton Santiago had placed yet another one of his strong pineapple and rum concoctions on the table next to my chair. I had not ordered it, but I decided immediately not to complain. Everton had determined that I needed another one and I felt forced to oblige him. Of course, I was not sure that I could get another down without going headfirst into a rum-induced, afternoon coma nap. I picked it up and felt the cold condensation from the glass drip onto my chest as I took a drink.

I put down the glass and picked up my iPhone. I held it out in front of my eyes to try to focus as I clicked to my Facebook home page. I began tapping away on the screen with my index finger. It took me a couple of times to clear my head enough to spell all the words correctly, but I finally finished my new status. "What ever happened to back alleys?" I hit the update button, closed my eyes and slumped back in the lounge chair.

I have always liked to start rhetorical discussions on Facebook. Usually these discussions revolved around my small town upbringing. This day, I chose my topic as alleys. Old, small towns have them and the cookie-cutter subdivisions of today do not. I believe the demise of modern society began when architects began planning neighborhoods without back alleys.

On the busted concrete of the narrow alleys of our youth, we found our generation. As kids, we used those alleys to walk home from school during the week and to walk to football games and school dances on the weekends. It is where we kissed our girfriends for the first time. And it is there where we fought to defend their honor. Across alleys our moms shared recipes and our fathers shared Wiedemann beer. It was the place where conversations took place on everything from politics to sports. The Viet Nam War was fought in alleys across the country. President Lyndon B. Johnson said the war was lost when Walter Cronkite called the conflict unwinnable. It was ultimately the debates in the alleys of small towns that LBJ was talking about. My dad watched Cronkite, as did the other dads who engaged in alley talk. When Cronkite told them the war could not be won, those dads believed him over the President.

Not that the robust debates in the alleys were always a good thing. Often, there were repercussions, especially for the children of the participants. There were certain expectations for those who grew up in a place where everyone knew everyone else's business. For better or worse, I was no exception and a child of that environment.

My destiny was decided for me in the alley behind my house. My options were few. While I longed to be my uncle, fishing my life away in the Everglades, it was determined for me that I was the one who was supposed to be successful. Good in school, polite in adult company, and thoughtful in life did not lead me to the career path of Renaissance Man. No matter what I wanted, my resume was written by the time I hit high school. There was no pamphlet for gambling and carousing on the wall in the Guidance Counselor's office. I looked. Believe me, I looked. Success was chosen for me. I was to be the one destined to find life beyond the flood wall.

Of course, like so many young people, I initially rebelled against my presumed destiny of success, using the back alley as the place to drink beer, smoke pot, and cop a feel under my girlfriend's bra. My rebellion was for naught. The demographics of small towns disallow denying one's personal manifest destiny. It was preordained that I was to escape. Everyone in town knew it and encouraged my getaway. My parents expected it. My teachers wanted to take credit for it.

Planning by the adults made for a unique relationship amongst the progeny. Those destined for success were reluctantly accepted by the various social strata of high school – jocks, stoners, popular kids – but never really made members of those societies. Those from whom little was expected in life reluctantly accepted their designation, but I suspect they resented those who had made those determinations for them. One day, the mother of a girl caught her daughter giving me a hand job and scolded her daughter, not me. I think she would have taught her daughter how to blow me if she thought it would have ensured a ticket out and a better long-term income potential.

It is what is to be expected of a town that had the same number of stop lights as council persons – six – and probably three times as many bars. There were two Catholic churches (one for the Irish and one for the Germans). There were also two of everything else – drug stores, lawyers, doctors and funeral homes. In regard to those secular services, those who used which service provider were generally divided along Protestant and Catholic lines.

In my adult years, parishioners tried to merge the two Catholic churches. But the Germans would not sit with the Irish. And the Irish had similar ill feelings about the immigrants kneeling next to them. The experiment failed and today all those who follow Vatican Two go to church in neighboring communities.

There were bars on every corner in the three block downtown shopping district and others sprinkled throughout the city – not a surprising phenomenon for a town split mainly along German and Irish lines. Interestingly, it turned out that people were more picky about who they sat next to in church than in bars. The Catholics (German and Irish alike) sat and drank with the Protestants. It happened that alcohol abuse professed no particular religious preference, except the Baptists in town were not allowed to partake – at least, not in front of each other. Consumption of alcohol was a common thread that held the community together. Even if there had been stringent zoning laws at the time, drinking would always be considered a non-conforming use for any property.

Most of the bars in town opened at 5 a.m. to accommodate the men who worked the third shift on the Southern Rail Road, the town's largest employer. We were not a traditional "Company Town" owned lock-stock-and-barrel by the Southern, but we were not far from it either. On their way home from the rail yard, those on the red-eye shift would stop by their favorite watering hole for a beer and an egg. Racing forms would be waiting for them just in case they wanted to place a bet with the in-house bookie. Some of the kids whose dads worked on the railroad would stop by on their way to school to pick up lunch money. We would all pitch pennies or flip baseball cards in the alley while our buddy would head in the bar's back door. A few minutes later he would come out with lunch money for himself and Slim Jims for everyone as an extra snack during study hall.

Today, social services would take kids away from parents handing out early-morning beef snacks in bars. Back then, hard-working men giving lunch money to their kids was considered a virtue, no matter where the transaction was consummated. We did not have Head Start and free breakfasts. We had Slim Jims in the alley behind the Stag Café.

Every bar had its regular customers. Gator and Angel liked the Rock Bar. Our neighbor went to The Stag. Still others hung out at the Buffalo Bar, Old Oak Café or the Starlight. One day, when my dad was dying and on his last leg, he asked me to go settle up with John T., a.k.a. the "Mole," who had transferred his bookie business to the Starlight after the Rock Bar was torn down. Apparently, my old man had a running account with the Mole in his later years. Without my mom's knowledge, he had been placing bets with the Mole on a regular basis. I was afraid how much he owed. So I went to the Starlight and told John T. that Angel was on his last leg and I needed to settle up with him. The Mole went into the back room, came out about fifteen minutes later and gave me $21.63. Even the bookie in our town was honest. It was enough money for me to buy a round for everyone at the Starlight in my dad's honor and still cover the tip.

Alleys were more than just teenage hangouts. Alleys sometimes divided the "bad" portions of town from the "good" ones – the houses to the north where the more respectable people lived from those to the south where lesser ne'er-do-wells who might be one step away from what Grandma would call "living down the road."

I recently read a news story about a kid I grew up with who was busted for cooking meth. He was still living on the same south-side street where he grew up. I read the story in the lobby of my family doctor as I was about to request a prescription of Ritalin for my "attention deficit" issues. In a small town, like the difference between bathtub meth and prescription speed, there's a fine line between success and failure.

Despite occasional deviations into life on the south side of the alley, my life was lived in the houses on the north side. And I had come to grips with that fact. Uncle Al – Gator – was the black sheep of the family who went to the "south side of the alley" as a matter of personal choice and never returned. My family was appalled when I talked about following in his footsteps. They made sure I walked a path more appropriate – a path that has haunted me my entire life.

Reflecting on the story in the *Miami Herald* made me realize there was one alley I still needed to conquer – Alligator Alley. And I was in South Florida. Alligator Alley was within driving distance. With the road starting out somewhere between Ft. Lauderdale and Miami, I could get there in just over an hour. Even in my drunken stupor, I realized I had to go – a personal and perfect homage to my Uncle Al.

With the groggy plan for the next day set, the last sip of Everton's latest drink made my eyes heavy. I thought for a moment about heading for my room, but I opted to close my eyes while sitting in the lounge chair by the pool. The warmth of the sun won out over the cool air conditioning of my room.

As I closed my eyes, I started to think about how much Florida had changed since my mom and dad had first visited here in the 50s. In the years before the Mouse became the leader of the Sunshine State, Florida was still a wilderness. Mom-and-pop hotels lined the Ft. Lauderdale beachfront and the Elbow Room was the place to go to have a beer. The beaches were nearly uninhabited and littered at the high-tide mark with seaweed. I remember my mother wanted to go shopping at Burdines one day, but changed her mind when she read in the newspaper that someone had been bitten by an alligator that had wandered downtown from a nearby canal. All the causeways were wooden drawbridges and the "boondocks" were less than a mile or two inland.

The trip to the Everglades when I was a young man seemed like it lasted forever. It would again this time, too. Maybe it was just nervous anticipation. I could not wait until tomorrow. I closed my eyes and succumbed to Everton's evil concoction.

*   *   *

Dust clouded up from behind the old blue Chevrolet Impala as Angel pulled the car into the parking lot off the dirt and gravel road. Jimmy had been watching the signs and billboards all the way down Alligator Alley indicating the Seminole Indian reservation was approaching. He read out loud to his little sister as they passed signs indicating that tourists could see men wrestle alligators and women weave blankets on authentic looms. The signs for the reservation were as frequent as those warning drivers to drive carefully.

When the car pulled up, Gator was standing by a chickee with a thatch roof. His thick glasses were nearly hidden under his sweat-stained, African-style, safari hat. Hadjo stood at Gator's side, looking as decrepit as the old man himself. Gator smiled and waved for Angel to park the car by him. "You're early," Gator proclaimed as he looked at his watch. "I thought you were leaving at noon."

It was hot and the air was musty. The tires made crunching noises as the car moved slowly over the shell gravel to a parking place.

"We did," Angel replied out the open window. "But we made great time out of Ft. Lauderdale." He turned off the car, stepped out and firmly shook Gator's hand. "The last 20 miles or so we were ballin' the jack."

Gator paused and made a quick calculation in his head of how fast Angel had been driving. "Damn," he said with manly respect. "That's pretty damn good for that stretch of road, atta boy."

"Hi, Uncle Albert," Jimmy's mom walked around the car and kissed Gator on the cheek. She had received Gator's letters explaining he had cancer, but she was shocked at his withered appearance. He was rail thin and his clothes hung loosely on his body. He looked much sicker than she had expected. As she spoke, she fought back tears. "You've lost a lot of weight. How do you feel?" she whispered.

"Hi, babe," Gator replied, leaning down and kissing the head of Jimmy's two year old sister. "I have good days and bad days ... not sure how many of either I have left." He patted her on her belly. "How many months until Jimmy gets another playmate?"

"A few," came Mom's blushing reply.

"And where is my favorite nephew?" Gator called out, adjusting his thick black glasses as he spoke. "Come on over here boy and let me take a look at ya."

Jimmy walked up to his great uncle and stood proudly. It had been years since he had seen his idol and he was excited to show him just how much he had grown. The old man was thinner than he remembered and looked frail.

"Damn," Gator exclaimed, looking the boy up and down. "You're gettin' big."

"Albert!" Jimmy's mom was used to Gator's frequent salty language, but felt compelled to complain nevertheless. "Language."

Gator waved his hand dismissively at the complaining woman. "Aw, hell," he said. "I bet he hears worse than that at school."

A stout Seminole woman walked over to the family. She was much younger than Gator and avoided eye contact with the family. Her hair was pitch black, with brightly painted peyote beads laced into her braids. "Folks, you remember me tellin' ya about Tayanita, don't ya?"

Jimmy's mother and father responded in unison with an uncomfortable evasion of their collective eyes. "Hmph," mumbled Gator with a furrowed brow while shaking his head. "Tayanita, please take my family down to my boat to get them a drink of water. If Angel wants a beer, there's some in the Frigidaire up in the main dining room." Gator put his arm around the boy. "Jimmy and I need to take a little walk."

"Don't let him get too close to those alligators," Jimmy's mom warned. She looked at her husband with a concerned expression. Angel nodded his approval of the excursion.

"Cut the apron strings and leave the boy alone," Gator shouted over his shoulder as he walked away with Jimmy. "He's going to be driving soon. He'll be fine."

"The cancer has made him more ornery than usual," Angel said to his wife as the pair walked with the Indian woman towards the house boat.

"I know," she replied. "I just hope Jimmy handles the news okay."

The old man and the boy started to walk down towards the river, casually talking about what fishing each had done since they had last seen each other. Jimmy talked quickly about a big catfish he caught out of the river with a homemade dough ball. Hadjo hobbled along at their side, struggling to keep up the same pace.

The trio stopped and looked at a man in an encaged pit, encircled by a wire fence and about a dozen onlookers. The man was staring into the eyes of an eight-foot alligator and was making half step advances as the alligator rocked from side to side on its haunches, hissing and growling at the man as he moved closer. In a quick move, the man leapt onto the back of the alligator and the two of them rolled around violently in the sand. After a short struggle, the man, breathing heavily, stabilized his weight on the animal's back. He gave the alligator a few seconds to calm down and then put both hands around its snout. Slowly, he bent the alligator's neck backwards and placed its closed mouth between his own chin and chest before removing his hands. The crowd applauded as he quickly let go and jumped off the alligator's back. The alligator let out a loud hiss and scurried away from the man.

"See that man, Jimmy?" Gator pointed at the man wrestling the alligator.

"Yes, sir," Jimmy replied.

"He knows something that you don't," Gator nodded.

"What's that, Unc?"

"All those folks watching and applauding think the man wrestling the alligator is putting on a show for them," he said as he pointed at the crowd.

"Isn't he?" Jimmy sounded confused.

"No, son," Gator smiled softly. "It's not about their entertainment. For the man on the alligator's back, it's a way for him to become a part of the alligator. Those people watching think he's conquering the animal. They don't understand that he's becoming a part of it."

Gator put his arm around Jimmy's shoulder and led him down towards the canal. They walked at a slow but deliberate pace. When they got to the water, Gator stopped, picked up a rock and tossed it into the Glades. He nodded at Jimmy to do the same thing. After Jimmy tossed his rock, Gator spoke. "This is the last time you'll see me, Jimmy."

"What? Why?" Jimmy looked up at Gator, stunned. "Are you going somewhere?"

"I'm sick, boy," he tilted his head and gazed out over the Everglades, "real sick ... the kinda sick ya never get over."

"No," Jimmy said. He was otherwise speechless. His face grew pale. In a moment, his head was spinning and he was unable to focus.

"Yup," Gator's voice was stern. "I'm about done here on earth."

Jimmy was shocked. He hoped one day to join his uncle on the reservation and learn how to hunt wild animals. They would live on the boat together and go fishing every day. Gator could not die. It would change everything. Jimmy's world was suddenly falling apart in front of him. "Can't the doctors do anything?" he stuttered in response. "Can't they make you better?"

Gator shook his head and crossed his arms. "I'm afraid not, son."

Jimmy tried to be strong and looked dead ahead as he fought back his tears. Seeing Jimmy's discomfort, Gator reached over and gently pulled the boy into his body. Jimmy put his head against the old man's shoulder and began to cry hard. He cradled Jimmy in his arms and rubbed his hair as he cried. Tears soaked through Gator's old white t-shirt and he could feel the moisture on his skin. Gator let him cry for awhile and held him as he did. When Jimmy calmed down, Gator looked down at him.

"Now I don't want no more crying over me, Jimmy," Gator instructed in a fatherly voice.

"But I don't want you to die," Jimmy pleaded, looking back up at Gator, wiping the tears off his cheeks. Self-pity was creeping in.

"Hell, son, neither do I, but we all gotta die," Gator laughed, trying to get the boy to smile. "Lots of folks do it in car wrecks and fires. I'm lucky. I know its coming and I'm gettin' to deal with it on my own terms. People die every day, but I get to know when."

"Why don't you come home with us?" Jimmy asked. "I bet the doctors back home could make you get better."

Gator smiled softly at the suggestion. He knew the boy wanted him to live and found it hard to explain that he was ready to go. "The Everglades is where I live, Jimmy," he said. He spread his arms wide as if to encompass the entire swamp and nodded as he spoke. "This is my home now," he affirmed. "A man needs to be in his own environment when his judgment day comes. I need to live the rest of my days here. Understand?"

"I guess so." Jimmy's reluctance showed in his voice.

"Besides," Gator continued, trying to sound strong and upbeat for the boy. "I'm doing what I love to do. My last day on this earth will be spent fishin' and playin' mandolin." He reached down and patted the dog. "And old Hadjo will be right by my side."

Jimmy wiped the tears from his cheeks, trying his best not to cry any more. "What about your guitar? Won't you be playing your guitar, too?"

"Nope," Gator replied, shaking his head.

"Why not?" Jimmy asked.

Gator looked down at the boy. "'Cause I'm givin' it to you."

Jimmy's eyes got wide. He knew Gator did not have many possessions and his Gibson Flattop guitar was one of his most prized. He gave Jimmy a kid's guitar one year for Christmas and taught him a few chords. They played a song together, but he would not let Jimmy play his Gibson. Jimmy's dad told him that Gator never let anyone play guitar. Jimmy was stunned his uncle was giving it to him. "I can't take your guitar," he said. "That's your favorite thing – next to Hadjo."

"Sure ya can," Gator smiled. He spoke softly now. "It is my favorite thing and, since you're my favorite nephew, I want you to have it."

Jimmy thought about the enormity of the gift he was being presented and relented to his great uncle's wishes. "I'll take real good care of it," he said. "I promise."

"I know ya will, boy," Gator replied. He reached over and ruffled Jimmy's hair. "Remember them chords I taught ya?"

"Yes, sir," Jimmy said. "C – D – G."

"Well, then," Gator said, "you know just about all the songs I ever sang to you. I'm gonna give it to you before you leave today. You take that old guitar and learn how to make it sing."

The pair stayed silent for a few minutes, looking across at an old cypress tree jutting up out of the water.

"Jimmy," Gator pointed the boy out towards the swamp. "See that out there?"

Jimmy nodded affirmatively, but not quite sure what his undle was pointing out. "I guess," he said.

"Over there, out in the swamp," Gator said, continuing to wave his hand. "When I die, Tayanita will find a proper resting place for me. Before she leads the tribe out to leave me there, she'll take all my remaining worldly possessions and toss them into the swamp."

"Why?" asked Jimmy.

"They don't want anything holding me back when my soul crosses over."

"Crosses over? To what?"

"Don't know," said Gator. He shrugged his shoulders. "Whatever's next, I guess."

They both stood silent for a minute, until Gator began to lead Jimmy back to his house boat. He pulled Jimmy close as they walked. "Anyway, I can't take my stuff with me. So when you leave today I want you to take my guitar and my best fishin' pole with ya."

*　*　*

"Hey, mon," Everton Santiago was gently nudging my shoulder as I opened and closed my eyes, trying to focus from my mid-afternoon rum drunk. "You better wake up."

"Your drinks should be by prescription only," I mumbled, rubbing my eyes. "They're better than any sleeping pill I've ever taken."

"Lots of people say that," Everton smiled widely.

I pulled myself to the side of the chair. "How long have I been out?" I pressed my index finger against my chest and looked at the impression to see if I was sun burnt.

Everton was placing several empty glasses on his tray. "A couple of hours, mon."

"Sorry," I mumbled as I stumbled up to my feet.

"No problem, mon. But you better get up to your room and get a shower. The party will be starting down here just after sunset. Come on down, mon and I'll introduce you around."

Chapter Four

Uncle Al and my old man, the Angel, took me into my first bar when I hit double digits. Sitting on a stool, drinking an RC made me feel mature – like I had come of age in my own time. Luckily for Dad, my mom never found out about that trip – not that she told me anyway. Lord knows, I never told her about it. It was a day forever etched in my mind. I sat at a barstool as an equal with my father and uncle. I was a man among other men. I might have been a child, but for me that deviled ham sandwich and soda pop made us peers. It also started my lifetime obsession with searching for the perfect watering hole.

Dad and Uncle Al liked the Rock Bar. Duke Bodkin and his brothers were their friends. The Bodkin boys went to a private Catholic school, rather than public school like my dad, but Duke was close to Dad's age. They lived on the same street growing up, so getting a drink at Duke's place just seemed natural. Gator liked going to Duke's because he always kept a bottle of Bostonian Rock-and-Rye on the shelf. And, whenever an angry wife called searching for a wayward husband, Duke covered for any man covering his tab.

One time, my little sister fell into a window well and cut her head so badly that she needed stitches. Mom called the

Rock Bar looking for Dad and, of course, Duke lied and said he had not seen him. Grandpa drove past the bar on his way to the hospital and saw Angel's Chevy parked out front. There was certainly hell to pay that night. Mom never again called the Rock B ar asking for Dad – she called and demanded to speak to him.

When the Rock Bar was torn down in order to build a new bank on the site, Angel and Gator started going to the Stag Cafe. Bud Crowley owned the Stag and it was the first drinking establishment on the west side of the city's main drag. The bar itself was U-shaped with beer taps and shelves of liquor running down the center of the opening. The building had large storefront windows, but they were painted halfway up so that people on the street could not look inside and see who was getting drunk. And, as the name indicated, the Stag was a men's only establishment. Women were not welcome – and, remembering the general conditions of the place and the demeanor of the patrons, I do not think women would have wanted to be there anyway.

Bud and his family were from upstate New York. One year Bud's brother, Lew, came to town on Derby weekend to visit. Lew parked the car in front of the bar, popped a nickel in the meter and headed inside to spend the day with his brother. After downing a few beers, Lew asked Bud where he could lay down a bet on the Run for the Roses.

Bud gave Lew directions to The Starlight, a competitor's bar located a few blocks away, just across the street from the police station. He instructed Lew to go inside and ask for "the Mole." Bud said, "tell 'em you're my brother." Lew headed up the street, followed his brother's instructions and got his bet down with plenty of time to spare before post time.

On his walk back to the Stag, Lew noticed that his parking meter had expired and a parking ticket had been placed under his car's windshield wipers. He took the ticket and walked back up the street to the police station in order to pay the fine. Unbeknownst to Lew, the city clerk had asked the Mole to sit at her window while she was out at lunch. When Lew appeared at the police station to pay his fine, the Mole was sitting behind the clerk's window.

Later that night, following the Kentucky Derby, Lew, Bud, and the entire Crowley family went to Saturday night mass. When the collection plates were passed from pew to pew, who should happen to be in charge of the row of Catholic Crowleys … the Mole.

When they left the church, Lew was bewildered. He had placed a bet with the Mole, paid a city parking ticket to him and made a proper tithe to him as well. When they got clear of the church, Lew turned to Bud and asked, "How much is this town in to the Mole for?"

Inspired by stories like those that had been relayed to me by my dad and Uncle Gator, the search for the perfect bar became my life's quest. When I was young, the quest revolved around drinking. And I drank a lot. I suspect that some would say I drank too much. But I never got a DUI or missed a day of work from booze or ended up having a child with some barmaid. God gave me a strong personal constitution for alcohol, and I took full advantage of it. I could stay up late drinking hard and go to work the next day no worse for the wear – a bad personality trait for someone who enjoyed drinking and carousing. As for the no children part—well, let's just call it karma.

The bars of my youth were wild places with sticky floors, drunk women, and loud live bands, where nearly anything could, and often did, happen.

As I got older, my search criteria for the perfect bar changed, along with my drinking habits. It was not the alcohol that started to get to me, but the way my aging body metabolized the sugar. Following a good drunk, my eyes would pop open around 4:00 a.m. Early mornings spent watching the ESPN Sports Center loop became more than I was willing to pay for my late night escapades. I could still knock back like I was young, but I could only do it one night in a row.

The fact that my drinking habits had changed, however, did not stop my quest for the perfect bar. I quit looking for the bar that mixed the best Manhattan and started looking for that place Gator had talked about that very first day at Duke's Rock Bar. I wanted to find a place where I did not have to put on airs. I wanted to sit back and instinctively feel at ease. The bar at the Ocean Reef Club certainly had its airs, but Everton Santiago had made me feel relaxed and comfortable. He was a good bartender – friendly and unassuming. I was not as sure about the evening party he had described and had encouraged me to attend.

The Florida sun had already set when I walked onto the pool deck and where just a few hours before I had taken my rum soaked power nap. A freshly caught, blackened swordfish steak and conch fritters seemed to have soaked up most of the rum remaining in my belly. I had that lightheaded feeling one gets when the buzz is gone, but the body is awaiting instructions to either stop or start over. My sugar buzz was calling out for more of the same. The fresh smell of a storm blowing in from the Gulf side was telling me to go back to my room early. The decision to stay or go was a very close call.

I had enjoyed my afternoon over indulgence. I did not drink heavily very often anymore, especially so early in the day. A part of me was crying out to complete the marathon. However, I had made up my mind to get up early the next morning and head over to the Everglades. I did not want a 4:00 a.m. sugar wake up call throwing me off my schedule. So, ignoring the inner demons tempting me with more dark rum, I decided in this instance one quick nightcap and an early return to the room was the better part of valor.

I slowly sauntered to the bar where I had imbibed during my earlier drinking session. The ambiance of the pool deck had definitely changed. The children in orange swimmies were gone and had been replaced by middle aged couples dressed in island apparel – men in khaki shorts and polo shirts with logos from exclusive golf resorts; women in sun dresses, spray-on tans and push up bras. Several of the men at the bar carried themselves with a mistaken attitude that the women around them were somehow more interested in the size of their cocks than the thickness of their wallets.

The friendly bartender from my afternoon bender, Everton Santiago, had been replaced by a young brunette who served me a nice after-dinner wine and directed me to another bar at the far end of the property where Everton was serving drinks for the evening.

I strolled along the bush-lined walkway, sipping at my glass of wine, when my cell phone rang. I looked at the caller identification. It was my wife, Veronica. She had not called since I left. In the back of my mind I wondered if she had wanted me out of her way for the week for more than just a business meeting. I considered letting it go through to voicemail.

"Happy birthday, babe," her voice had a tone to it that rang of false adulation.

"Missed it by a day," I replied in a nonchalant voice. I spied a bench, sat down and placed the glass of wine on the ground. "I thought that I'd hear from you yesterday."

"Yeah, well, about that," she stuttered. "I'm really sorry for not calling yesterday, but my dinner with Paul and our new clients went way late. I was afraid that if I called, I'd wake you up."

I did not believe her. She and Paul had been having a lot of late night meetings lately. Still, I did not want to start an argument long distance. Sadly, it really was not worth the frustration. I spent so many years masking my anger with other emotions, it was, in fact, hard to determine just what I was feeling about the call. "It's okay," I replied. "I hit the sack pretty early last night anyway."

"So what have you done so far?"

"When I got into Miami yesterday," I replied, keeping my voice low so people walking by could not hear our conversation. "I hung around the dog track for awhile before coming to the resort."

"Win anything?"

"I came out ahead," I replied.

"You usually do." She seemed to be asking questions as if on auto-pilot. "How about the hotel? Is it as nice as advertised on the web site?"

"Yeah," I complimented. "You picked a really nice place. Today I just lounged around the pool, sipping rum drinks, and listening to some guy play tunes."

"Sounds like you're unwinding," Victoria said.

"Oh yeah," I said. "This place is really relaxing." I considered my next words carefully. I ignored the bravado instructing me to remain silent and spoke anyway. "I wish you were here with me. You'd really like this place."

"Maybe someday," Victoria sounded strikingly non-committal. "So what's on the schedule for tomorrow?"

"I think I'm going to put the top down on the rental car, drive up to the 'Glades and look around a bit. The bartender here at the place knows where I can get an airboat ride through the swamp. I'm not sure, but I think it's out by where my uncle used to live."

"Your mom's crazy old Uncle Gator?" she replied. I winced. I always called him crazy, but felt uncomfortable when others did so. "Well, that sure sounds like fun."

"Yeah," I smiled to myself. "I brought Gator's fishing pole with me. I may even wet a line after the boat ride."

"Just try to relax while you're out there. You need it."

"Yeah, I will."

After some more idle chat, we ended the conversation. It was a bad call for both of us. A text would have expressed more emotion. I stuffed the phone in my pants pocket, living with the pitiful admission that whatever we seemed to be lacking these days was probably my fault more than hers. I met Victoria following the demise of my first marriage. She was pretty and possessed the one characteristic I was searching for – a strong libido. Victoria had always enjoyed sex just as much as I did. The start of my discontent seemed to coincide with a corresponding disinterest in sex by Victoria, I surmised. She probably found it difficult to remain passionate for a man who had lost his own passion for life.

I hoped this vacation was going to reinvigorate the passion in both of us – me for life, her for me. I was crushed when she cancelled, but was determined to do my part and return to her with a spring in my step. I knew my confidence had eroded over the past several years. I was not the same guy she married. If I could figure out what happened and fix it, maybe that alone would cause Victoria to rethink how she felt about me.

What better way to start than at a bar. I walked over to the station where Everton was serving drinks.

"Hey, mon," Everton said, his ever present smile welcoming me to his bar. "You were pretty red this afternoon. You're looking a lot better than when I saw you a few hours ago."

I laughed at Everton saying I was red, Jamaican slang for drunk. "Amazing what some food and a cold shower will do to neutralize a good red."

Everton pointed at the lineup of top shelf liquor behind the bar. "Want another rum drink?"

"Oh, no way, Everton," I said raising my glass of wine. "I'm just going to have a glass or two of wine and head in early."

"That doesn't sound like very much fun." The soft voice came from a tanned dishwater blond in an off-white sun dress sitting alone at the bar. I could not understand why I hadn't noticed her when I walked up to Everton's station. I should have. She was damn attractive. When Everton told me earlier there would be pretty women around in the evening, he might have been thinking of her.

"It isn't," I responded with a stiff smile. "But I had too much fun today. I think I bought stock in a rum company owned by Everton's family."

She nodded at Everton. "Then I'll drink for both of us. Everton, give me a double vodka and tonic." She patted the seat next to her, inviting me to sit down. "I'm Lilith."

"Hi," I reached out my hand as I sat down. "I'm James."

Lilith softly shook my right hand, but her eyes were clearly focused on my left hand, in particular, my wedding ring. "What brings you to Key Largo, James?" Her voice was almost taunting me as she tilted her head. "Family vacation?"

"His birthday, mon," Everton interjected. He reached over and patted me on my shoulder. "My man James is here to celebrate his birthday."

"And yet you're at the bar by yourself?" Lilith cocked an eyebrow.

"Yeah," I replied. I looked down at the glass of wine I was swirling from side to side. "My wife had to stay behind for some damn business meeting. So, I came on down by myself for a little rest and relaxation."

"Too bad for her."

Lilith's voice seemed to imply *and good for me*. My temperature clicked up a notch. I was glad it was dark so no one could see me blushing. I had not been in this type of situation for years, and quite frankly I had forgotten what to do. As our conversation continued, everything about Lilith seemed to indicate she was coming on to me ... her voice, her body language ... everything. But it had not happened in so long, I was not sure. She pulled out a cigarette and held it out until I dug around in my pocket for my lighter. I lit her smoke and then pulled one out my pack. I noticed that my hand was shaking a little as I lit my own cigarette.

Lilith blew out a long puff of smoke and put her elbow up on the bar. "So, Birthday Boy," she said, "if you had your fun today, what do you intend to do for the rest of the night?"

"I'm not quite sure yet," I replied. Quite honestly, I was not sure. I had expected to have a quick glass of wine and head up to bed. Lilith had changed things. I had not had a woman other than my wife express sexual interest in me for years. My wife, Victoria, and I had an active sex life. However, as our call had reminded me, I had begun to wonder if it was out of mutual attraction or common convenience that we fucked. For the moment, it was exhilarating to think that a woman I never met before was making a move on me. But, because my hardening dick was quickly responding in kind, it was also scary. I wanted a change of pace for the week, but this was something I had not considered.

On one hand, my wife had dumped me on my birthday. I was here alone because she stayed behind. She had put me in this situation. Not that she would ever know. So maybe I should head back to the room with Lilith for spite. Victoria wanted me to have a good time – fuck it – I should have a good time. Still, I am not that kind of guy. In the end, I would probably feel so guilty it would spoil the rest of the vacation. I did not need that kind of drama this week.

I punted.

"I think that I'm going to finish up my wine and call it an early night," I said as I got up from my barstool. "I'm getting up pretty early in the morning to head up to the 'Glades."

"Come on and sit back down," Lilith urged. "Have another glass of wine." She reached out and touched my hand. It was contact that, although ever so slight, felt more electric than any I had ever experienced. It sent a wave of primal desire through my body. She looked directly at the uncomfortable bulge growing in my pants and then up into my eyes. She smiled coyly. "What could it hurt?"

I quickly gulped down the rest of my wine and put the empty glass on the bar. "I think I'm going to head up to my room." I nodded my retreat. "Goodnight."

"I'll be here if you change your mind," Lilith said.

As soon as I turned and started to walk away, doubt began to creep in. Here I was alone on a small island with an attractive woman and I was walking away. I probably could take her up to my room for a glorious night of sex and no one, including my wife, would ever be the wiser. It took all of my willpower to keep walking towards the hotel entrance. Twice I slowed down and nearly stopped, but forced my legs to continue forward.

As I got to the door, I paused. My feet seemed to be set in concrete along with my moral dilemma. I closed my eyes and gritted my teeth at the decision – stay or go. Then I remembered what Everton had told me about the women that frequented his bar. They were looking for men that had just as much to lose as them. I shook my head as I wondered if Lilith would be as attracted to me if she realized just how little I had to lose. I stepped inside and headed to my room.

*   *   *

The small wood frame house was not built to hold as many people as actually lived under its tin roof. But times were hard and the family had figured out a way to make the cramped space work. The attic had been converted into a bedroom for Jimmy's parents and his baby sister. Jimmy continued to sleep on the army cot in his grandma's room, just off the first-floor kitchen. He was in bed one night staring at the pictures he had taped on the wall. As he listened to the sound of his father shoveling coal cinders from the furnace in the basement, the phone rang. His mom picked it up and shouted through the register into the basement that the call was for Angel. Jimmy heard the cellar door close before his dad entered the back door and grabbed the phone from the desk. Angel looked in the direction of the open door to the bedroom. Jimmy closed his eyes quickly and pretended to be asleep. When his father turned, Jimmy opened his eyes and watched the drama unfolding in front of him.

"Slow down, Louella," Angel said into the phone. Louella was Gator's wife and Jimmy's great aunt. "I can't understand a thing you're saying." He listened for a moment and then said, "Honey, I've not seen Gator since we went fishing last Saturday. I don't know where he is."

Jimmy's grandma walked into the room. The stable matriarch of his mother's side of the family, she was old and frail, but her word ruled the house. She was always dressed proper in a flowered dress of some sort with a sweater around her shoulders no matter the weather. She stared at Angel as he spoke on the phone. She had a concerned look on her face. Angel shrugged his shoulders.

Angel's eyes got large and then narrowed. It looked like he was trying to fight back a laugh. Then he shook his head as he spoke. "Well, what the hell did you tell him that for?" Apparently, Louella tried to explain something else to Angel, but he cut her off. "Look, Louella, it's late and I'm tired. I'll ask around town in the morning, but right now I'm going to bed. I suggest that you do the same thing. Good night."

"What's wrong?" Grandma asked frowning. "What did Louella want? Is Gator okay?"

Angel shook his head. "Apparently, Louella gave Gator an ultimatum."

"An ultimatum? About what?"

"Louella told Gator he had to decide between her and the fish."

"Oh, dear Lord," Grandma's voice trailed off. "What was she thinking? Gator's halfway to Florida by now."

Chapter Five

The headline in the daily newspaper, *The Kentucky Post*, was one of the most spectacular that the community had ever seen –

'Big Game Hunt' on for 'Gators in Devou

A full-scale "big game hunt" was in progress Wednesday in Devou Park, Covington, as police and park employees searched for two alligators that escaped from their tank in the Behringer Museum on Tuesday.

The alligators were reported to have been seen in Prisoner's Lake a short distance from the museum Tuesday night.

Bobby McCabe, superintendent of the park, said he had instructed his men to keep a close watch on the lake in the event the alligators make their appearance again.

Hope for Capture

Mr. McCabe said if the reptiles are seen again, he will request Albert ('Gator) Clarke, who gave the alligators to the museum a week ago, to recapture them.

One is five feet long and the other is three feet.

Ellis Crawford, curator of the museum, said the alligators escaped from a metal tank in which they were being kept until permanent quarters could be made for them.

Police, under Captain James Chastain, located the alligators in the lake a short time before the weekly Devou Park Community Sing Association concert was held in the park amphitheater.

Mr. Clarke, though the innocent cause of the Devou Park excitement Tuesday night, is the envy of virtually every lover of wildlife.

While here during the summer months, Mr. Clarke, a carpenter and contractor, lives in Bromley. In the fall, he lives in the Florida Everglades where he devotes his time to his profession, carpentering, as well as hunting and fishing.

Gets Quail, Too

When not on his big game hunts for alligators and wild boar, 'Gator finds time to snag a few bass in a nearby river. His catch usually brings him at least six bass, weighing an average of five to six pounds.

If he wants a few quail or doves, he merely sits about quietly near his home and can bag the limit within a short time.

While a builder and a contractor some years ago, Mr. Clarke now devotes his time to remodeling work when here, and then – off to Florida for more fishing and hunting and some work to squeeze in when he finds the time.

He plans to leave next week for the Everglades to pursue his favorite pastime, but some of the folks who like to visit Devou Park are hoping he doesn't bring back any more live alligators.

*   *   *

Over the years, I told many people about the great Kentucky alligator hunt. The funny thing was, very few ever actually believed my story. I had to show people the article from the newspaper to get them to buy into it. Even after reading the newspaper article, most remained skeptical. The thought of alligators roaming the woods of a Kentucky park seemed quite a tall tale, even when backed by journalistic news clips. The story was part of Gator's local legend.

Before Gator took off for good, he would go fishing and hunting every year in Florida. He would always come back with more than just a truck full of Indian River fruit. Usually, the extra load consisted of stories about tracking wild game that he would weave for the boys at the local bars. Occasionally, he would bring back a snakeskin or a stuffed alligator head. One year, he brought back something a little more tangible – two alligators for Billy and Tommy, the sons of his best fishing buddy, Rudy Gaither.

The Gaither boys were enthralled by their new pets and had every intention of keeping them. They dug a pit in back of their house on Carneal Street and put chicken wire around the hole. They started charging kids in the neighborhood a nickel a piece to come and look at the alligators. A steady flow of kids – and adults – made their way to the Gaithers' backyard. The enterprise came to an end when Mrs. Gaither tried to push the alligators back into the pit with a broom and the larger of the pair bit the handle in two. The collected admission having not covered the cost of a new Fuller Brush broom, the Carneal Street Alligator Park abruptly closed its doors to the animal loving public.

Gator and Rudy decided to give the alligators a new home at a local museum that had a collection of stuffed animals, fossils, local artifacts and oddities, including a stuffed two-headed calf. They put the two reptiles in temporary cages and went about building permanent, more secure, quarters. On the third day of construction, Gator and Rudy showed up to the museum to find the temporary cages empty. The alligators were gone. A search of the museum grounds turned up nothing. Rudy and Gator assumed they had been stolen. Later in the day, police headquarters began getting phone calls about alligators roaming around the park's golf course. After a thorough investigation, the police knew who to call.

Gator quickly fessed up to being the man responsible for alligators tormenting the golfers of Devou Park and promised the Chief of Police he and Rudy would catch them.

Word spread quickly throughout the community about the escapade and people began searching the park for the scaly escapees. They found them in Prisoner's Lake, an old rock quarry dug by inmates of the county jail and later filled with water. About a hundred people lined the shore of Prisoner's Lake where the two ultimate fishermen went about catching the pair of alligators. It was quite a scene. Gator went out on the lake in a canoe and lured the first gator to the surface with some raw chicken. When the first alligator emerged for the fresh meal, Gator was able to catch a treble hook under one of its stubby legs. Rudy stood on the shore with a square fiberglass Wright Magill rod-and-reel struggling to get the animal to the shore. When he was within range, Gator jumped from the canoe into the lake and onto the alligator's back. He grabbed a hold of the animal's jaw. Rudy took some electrical tape and wrapped it around the alligator's snout. It thrashed back and forth as Gator and Rudy dragged it onto the shore and carried it to the pickup truck.

Rudy tossed the exhausted animal into Gator's old pickup truck and then they went about catching number two. It was smaller, but much quicker. It took Gator a bit longer to hook him. But once he was hooked, bound, and tossed into the back of the truck with his fellow traveler, a roar went up from the crowd. The men and boys tossed their hats in the air. Newspaper photographers caught it all for the morning edition.

The next day the local newspaper published a photo of Rudy struggling with the bent fiberglass rod to get the animals to the shore. Rudy sent the photograph to the manufacturer of the rod and they sent him a whole bunch of free gear. They used the photo in their advertisements for years with the caption "Tough Enough to Catch Alligators in Kentucky."

All the kids gathered around the pickup truck and got to touch the alligator's rough, spiny skin. Rudy and Gator told everybody they were going to give the captured pair to the Cincinnati Zoo. However, as an adult, I went to the museum where it all started and saw a stuffed alligator displayed on the wall that looked awfully familiar. I had trouble looking it in the eye.

*   *   *

The midnight rain storm caused the morning air to smell clean and fresh as the wind whipped through my rented red Ford Mustang convertible. Everton's directions had been right on the mark and a thrill rushed through my veins as I pulled onto the stretch of road known simply as Alligator Alley, a concrete connection between the east and west coasts of South Florida – and hopefully a connection between me and my youth. Clouds hung so low to the ground

I felt as though I could reach out and grab them with my hand.

I was not quite sure what I was expecting as I opened up the engine and looked out at a storm forming miles north in the distance. It was not as if I had spent a large part of my childhood here. In fact, I had only been out to see Gator on the reservation once, right before he died. I was a youngster and my dad had done all the driving. There are several reservations in South Florida and I was not even sure which one we had visited back then. Still, a portion of my personality was formed somewhere along my own romantic imagery of the Everglades – saw grass and cypress trees, alligators and Indians. My mind spun in anticipation.

If I was going to find myself, Alligator Alley seemed like the likely place to start. As Gator used to say, "Every good adventure begins with a bad decision."

As I drove, I was hoping there would be some sign, or some mental reminder that pointed to the tourist stop near where Gator had lived. No such luck. The old signs counting down the number of miles to men wrestling alligators were gone. Alligator Alley, once a dangerous and lonely two-lane road was Interstate 75 now – just another part of America's interstate highway system. Back then, I can remember Mom and Dad packing supplies in the car in case we broke down. Even from the start, my drive indicated that Alligator Alley was not too different today from any other major road I had traversed in recent years.

In a day gone by, the drive across Alligator Alley was a high adventure fraught with the fear of either slipping off the road into a canal filled with deadly water moccasins or getting eaten by an alligator while changing a flat tire. Now, the deep-water canals formed from the steam-driven dredges that built up the roadbeds are protected by tall chain link fences that keep the cars out of the water and the wildlife away from the road. Swamp critters pass under the road in government-built tunnels.

I pulled over at a scenic rest stop and looked out at the saw grass and palmetto trees. But with cars zooming past on a major freeway behind me, I failed to grasp the vastness of the Everglades. Even the alligator frolicking thirty feet away in the canal did not seem all that menacing. I suddenly had a fatalistic view of my trip. The mystical beauty of the Everglades as I remembered it had succumbed to progress – four paved lanes of it to be precise. Maybe I should not have ventured away from the confines of the resort. Perhaps I just should have left well enough alone. Sometimes your recollections can be far more exciting than the truth. I got back into the car and begrudgingly proceeded on my journey.

Nothing changed in my trip as I drove the distance from east to west with absolutely nothing at all jarring my memory. At a gas station, I looked at a map and decided to head south down State Route 29 to the Tamiami Trail. Alligator Alley had done nothing for me. Maybe the "old" route connecting east and west would be a bit more scenic.

As I headed south towards the Tamiami Trail, my mind wandered to the events surrounding my morning cup of coffee. When I got up, I grabbed a cup of joe and walked down to a table on the concrete deck next to the small beach against the Atlantic Ocean. I sat down, lit up a cigarette and looked out at the vastness of the ocean. It was early and the sun was barely above the eastern horizon, casting a beautiful long white reflection across the calm water.

I ingested my morning dose of nicotine and caffeine as a young Hispanic worker in crisp white coveralls walked up to the beach with a rake. Slowly, he began taking his rake and pushing the sand up to the edge of the concrete border. Then, with meticulous precision, he pulled the rake backwards towards the ocean, eliminating the footprints from the day before and leveling out the sand. When one line was perfect and complete, he would start with another.

I sat and sipped gingerly at my coffee. I was mesmerized by the work of this young man and I was in no hurry to finish. I was fascinated at the professional manner by which he went about conducting a job that most folks would think of as mundane and unimportant. He leveled out the bumps made in the sand from the day before so people there today would wake up to find it perfect. Unaware of the man's efforts, those people would spend the entire day messing it up. Then, the next morning, he would again go about making the beach perfect again in a dance with tourists that was a part of his daily life. His work was a small effort that went unnoticed by most of the people who visited the beach. Somehow, it made me feel at peace.

As I drove south on State Route 29, the young man's efforts filled my mind. I had just driven across Alligator Alley expecting to find a memory from my childhood, and all I could think about was how my life had become all about pushing sand to make other people's lives perfect. I work in that infamous category of jobs known as "middle management." There are people I report to and people who report to me. In the middle, I level out the sand – making it perfect for them to do their respective jobs. Few rarely notice the effort.

From the standpoint of what had been predetermined for me in the alleys of my hometown, I was successful. I made a good salary for my efforts at a company well thought of in the community. Despite the expectations thrust upon me in my youth, I was coming to understand that smoothing out beaches for others to walk on was not really making me happy. Combined with the frustration of my drive across Alligator Alley, it was hammered home that I felt empty – unfulfilled. I could not remember when I last believed in anything of substance.

On top of the emotions about moving sand in my life, the drive across Florida had been personally disappointing, and I realized I was not really sure what I had been expecting. My anticipation at seeing Florida in the raw had been unrealistic. I should have expected the visuals of my youth to be gone. Despite how much I wanted things to be the same, they do change. The drive suddenly become a metaphor for my life – great anticipation followed by greater disappointment.

I should have expected the change. As was pointed out in the news article I read by the pool, the Seminoles derived their wealth from casinos now. They probably did not need the income from touristy road-side reservations to support the tribe. In the old days, the tribe ran games of Jackpot Bingo, sold tax-free tobacco products, and wrestled alligators to make ends meet. Now the Native American families get monthly checks from the corporations that run the casinos.

Still, despite the letdown of my westbound drive, I had to smile. The state route I was now on was revealing more of the uniqueness of the 'Glades to me. The fences separating the road from the canals were gone and I could look out and see much more of the natural beauty of the swamp. The canals were right against both sides of the two-lane road and filled with lily pads. I looked to the horizon on either side and could see clumps of cypress and palmetto trees peeking out of the saw grass in the distance. I began to notice the occasional house I passed along the way had at least one chickee on the property. Then I started noticing houses of concrete brick with chickee roofs. Just in front of a low shoulder warning sign, a coyote walked across the road in front of me. Memories of an older Florida were suddenly presenting themselves.

When I pulled up to the stop sign at the intersection of State Route 29 and Tamiami Trail, I looked out my window to see an alligator sunning himself not three feet from the road. This is what I had come for. I turned east onto Tamiami Trail with a huge smile on my face. As I drove, tourist stops for airboat and swamp buggy rides began to appear. I passed the "official" research center for Skunk Ape – the Everglades version of Big Foot. When I stopped for a snack at a small crab shack, I ate on a deck not 20 yards from an alligator peeking out of a canal.

The road trip across Alligator Alley that started as a bust had suddenly become a boon. I was in no hurry to get back to my hotel room, but jumped back into the car eagerly anticipating what might come next. My senses were nearing overload as I looked for gators on either side of the road. The closer I got to the Seminole reservation, the more roadside chickees began to appear with signs promoting genuine Indian trinkets and fresh grown fruit.

Then, I saw it – Gatorland Water Park. It was not like the place where my uncle had lived, which was a roadside front for an actual reservation. This place was a pure tourist trap. The main building was made of cement brick painted shell pink and the thatch lay on top of a tin roof to give the appearance of a chickee. The sign out front offered airboat rides, a snake show, and alligator wrestling. I pulled in, bought a ticket and began to wander around the grounds.

Around the back of the main building was the dock where the airboats were stationed. I proceeded there and handed my ticket to a young man dressed in jeans and a University of Florida t-shirt. His nose ring and tattoos screamed "cracker." Despite my obvious enthusiasm for the upcoming airboat ride, the youngster seemed quite disinterested in my patronage with his employer. I walked down the dock and joined a dozen others getting on a large airboat. Following some basic safety instructions, we placed noise reduction headsets over our ears and the boat moved slowly up a shallow canal. Alligator eyes popped up out of the water, glanced at the oncoming craft and disappeared again.

A second boat passed us on its way back into the dock. It was filled with laughing patrons, wet from the spray generated on the ride. And that was when I first noticed him. Everyone I had seen at the park thus far had been white. At the command of the returning boat was a tall and broad shouldered, darker-skinned man. His black hair was pulled back in a pony-tail, his face sweaty and emotionless. My eyes followed him as our boat passed his in the canal.

The boat ride was fun and loud. At one point, the kid with the nose ring put some raw meat on the end of a long stick and ran it back and forth a few times through the water. Then he held the bait a foot or two above the water and just waited. It did not take long before a large alligator jumped up and snatched the meat from the stick. Adults gasped and the kids screamed.

The man captaining the boat smiled. "Keep that in mind when we tell you to keep your hands inside the boat." Nose-ring boy looked up at the boat's captain, circled his finger in the air and shouted, "Let's head back in."

Once we were back at the dock, I waited and let all the other tourists get off the boat. The customers were excited and chatting amongst themselves about the wild boat ride they had just taken. I watched until they all cleared the boat and then stepped up to the edge of the dock. The dark-skinned man I had seen piloting the other craft was helping guests off our boat. When I went to get off the boat, he offered me his hand and hoisted me up. As he pulled me up from the flat hull of the boat, I asked bluntly, "You a Seminole?" I steadied myself on the dock and could tell he did not appreciate the forward nature of the question.

The young man withdrew his hand. He scowled at me and paused a moment before spitting some chewing tobacco juice into the water. "Who's askin?" he replied.

"I'm sorry," I said, realizing the tone of my question must have sounded a bit abrasive to the stranger. "That was a rather rude way to start a conversation." I tried to soften the expression on my face, but there was still no response from the man. I figured I had nothing to lose, so I decided to continue. "My name is James ... James Conrad." I stuck out my hand to try and renew our previous handshake. The young man reluctantly took my hand into his.

"Catori," he said as he looked around as if to see if someone was watching him. Once he decided he was outside of all public scrutiny, he continued. "But everyone here at this place calls me the Chief."

"Chief?" I responded. "Are you part of the Seminole tribal leadership?" I suddenly realized that my facial expression indicated that I was impressed at the thought.

"No," he chuckled sarcastically and shook his head. "But this place is run by wasichu."

"Wasichu?"

"White men," he grunted. "They call me Chief just because I'm a red man. They have no idea about tribal structure."

I thought for a minute. While I love calling people by their nicknames, Catori must have thought of his as a slur. "Mind if I call you Catori instead of Chief?" I asked as I stuffed my hands in my pants pockets.

The man smiled for the first time. I had made an inroad. "Catori works for me," he replied.

"Good," I said as we started to walk down the dock. I was pleased the young man had opened up, ever so slightly, to me. I decided to go for broke. "Catori, when I was a kid I once visited a relative of mine who lived out here in the 'Glades on an old Seminole reservation. It was kind of a tourist stop where people would come and watch men wrestle alligators and milk venom from the teeth of rattle-snakes ... stuff like that." I glanced at Catori as we walked. He was listening and engaged. "But it's also where the tribe lived."

"Yeah," Catori replied, nodding his head. "There aren't any of those places around anymore. My father told me they used to be all over the Everglades." He waved his hand across the horizon. "There are places all along Tamiami, but not too many Seminole work there anymore. They hire white men to wrestle the alligators now."

"Really?" I could tell Catori was bothered by the impli-cations. "And that troubles you?"

"They advertise it as authentic Seminole culture," Catori said, shaking his head. "But it's a bunch of white men put-ting on a show for other white men."

I thought about Catori's words and reflected on the les-sons my uncle had taught me about the art of alligator wres-tling. "Well, I'm sorry to hear about the change," I said. "This relative of mine I told you about, he was my uncle – well, great uncle, actually. He taught me alligator wrestling was about becoming one with the animal."

Catori smiled. "Your uncle was a wise man."

"Yes, he was," I replied. "I asked if you were a Seminole, because I was hoping that you might be able to help me locate that old tourist stop. Like I said, my uncle lived there with the tribe."

"Your uncle lived with the Seminoles?" Catori cocked his head in disbelief.

"Yeah." I realized that it was probably hard for a young Indian to comprehend that, back in the day, an old white man had lived with the tribe. Even though it was the truth, Catori did not look convinced.

"That was odd for the time," Catori said. He clearly was not buying my story.

"So I've been told," I replied. I realized I was nearing the end of my time with the young man. "But my uncle was kind of odd."

"Sorry, boss," Catori shook his head, "but that was long before my time."

My disappointment was clear on my face. "Damn," I said, nodding my head. "I guess it was crazy to think I could find it out here," I was mumbling to myself before realizing Catori was listening. There had been an edgy desperation in my voice as the memory I was searching for was weighing on me. I quickly changed my tone. "Thanks just the same." I closed my eyes, paused and sighed. Then I raised my chin, smiled softly and stuck out my hand. "Catori … it was a pleasure to make your acquaintance."

"You too, James." Catori must have read the disappointment on my face as he returned my handshake. As I started to walk away, I heard him from behind. "Hold on, James."

I turned. Catori was beaming. "Want to see a real Seminole wrestle an alligator?" He nodded his head towards a structure about 50 yards from the main building as an invitation.

"Yeah," I smiled back with a wide grin. "You bet your sweet ass I would."

Catori and I silently followed the signs indicating the large circular wall in front of us housed the alligator pit. The round enclosure had a sand island in the middle. The water in the front from where we approached was shallow, but in the back it was much deeper. At least a dozen alligators of various sizes lay motionless in the water. Two were on the sand island enjoying the early afternoon sun.

"Look at their backs," Catori instructed, pointing to one on the island. "You can tell the ones that have been here awhile from the ones we've just caught by looking at their backs."

"How so?" I squinted through my sunglasses at the alligators.

"See those spiny points sticking up on their backs?" Catori said.

"Yeah," I replied looking at the pair.

"Alligators kept here are well-taken care of and can live for up to 50 years in captivity," Catori continued. "The ones with pointy spines are new here, fresh caught from the Glades. The ones that have been here awhile have their skin smoothed down from having their buddies climb over them all day long."

The distinction was obvious when pointed out, but would not have been picked up by the casual observer. I looked at the various animals moving around in the pit. "So which one are you going to wrestle?"

"I like to wrestle the new ones," Catori said. "They have more fight in them." Catori looked at me and raised his eyebrows up and down in quick succession. He took off his shirt revealing a muscular upper frame. He twisted his neck around to loosen up and his spine made successive cracking sounds. I noticed he had multiple scars on his arms, but decided not to ask where they came from. He had a tattoo of a cypress tree on his massive right bicep. He cracked his knuckles, one hand at a time then said, "It's time to have some fun."

When Catori jumped on the wall, the alligators with the smooth backs quickly swam away to the deep end of the pit. Those on the island stayed put until Catori lowered himself into the shallow front water. Then as Catori approached, they turned and started to retreat to the sanctuary of the deep water as well. Before one of the "wild" ones could make it all the way back to the water, Catori grabbed it by the tail and pulled it back to the center of the sand island. The alligator thrashed back and forth as it was dragged backwards in the sand. The alligator hissed and let out a guttural growl that seemed to emanate from somewhere deep in its belly. A few other tourists began to congregate around the pit to watch.

Catori moved to the front of the alligator. "These guys are said to have very small brains," Catori said in a determined cadence, never letting his eyes stray from those of the gator. "But, then again, you don't have to be very smart to be a predator." Catori took a half step forward and the animal responded by moving a similar distance backwards. "For that, they have just the right amount of brain capacity."

"Got it," I said. My eyes were transfixed on the rhythmic movements between Catori and the alligator.

"Look at its eyes, James." Catori was still now.

"They're dark," I replied.

"Not that," Catori said somewhat frustrated that I was missing his point. "Look at the location."

I did as instructed. "Yeah."

"They are close together and in front of the jaw joint," Catori said, reaching for a walking stick that was partially buried in the sand. He grabbed the stick and held it out towards the animal's snout. "Once he opens his mouth, he's blind to the front. His eyes will be looking straight up at the sky. As soon I get him to smile, he's defenseless to anything I do in front of him."

"Okay," I nodded.

"So watch and learn." Catori thrust the stick at the alligator. The animal immediately opened up his massive jaws in a defensive move. The alligator sat there motionless with his mouth agape, growling. Just as Catori had said, his view to the front was blocked by a blind spot of its own making. Catori slowly walked up to the gator and carefully placed his fingers in the soft pocket of skin under the animals chin. The gator's mouth slammed shut and Catori quickly wrapped his thumb over the snout of the animal. Then in one motion he gently moved his other hand along his first, sliding both hands along the side of the jaws on the gator. Catori's eyes were riveted to the animal. "And now, as your uncle would say, we are one."

The people around the pit applauded.

Catori smiled. "Who are you applauding for?" He asked jokingly without looking our way. "Me or him?"

The people were all chuckling when Catori swung around to the animal's back. They immediately quit laughing and again fixed their gaze on the pair on the island. The animal struggled for a moment, kicking its short legs in the sand in an attempt to get traction. He spread the legs out making sure it could not get good footing. Once the animal had calmed a bit, Catori looked at me. "To be one," he said.

Catori brought the gator's closed snout up and trapped it between his own chin and chest. Once secure, ever so gingerly, he released his hands from the alligator's jaws and threw his arms out into the air. Again the people applauded. He returned his hands to the jaws before quickly placing a knee into the gator's back. Once he felt secure, Catori let go and leapt back. The animal hissed and quickly made its way to the deep end of the moat.

As Catori waded off the island into the shallow end, he looked at me and then the crowd. "And that is how you wrestle an alligator," he smiled. The tourists snapped pictures on their smart phones and cameras and applauded wildly.

Catori nodded his appreciation to the crowd as he walked up to me at the wall. "How about it, James?"

"That was great," I exclaimed, slowly clapping in sincere appreciation of Catori's skills.

Catori cocked his head. "You want to give it a shot?"

"Me?" I exclaimed in disbelief as I shook my head. "No way, my friend."

"You want to find your uncle," Catori coaxed. "I bet he wrestled alligators in his life."

"He had a bit of experience at it," I replied, again shaking my head.

"You search for the spirit of your uncle," Catori continued, nodding his head over his shoulder. "I can't guarantee that you will find him, but in this pit you may just capture a bit of his spirit."

I paused, silently surprised that I was actually contemplating Catori's offer to enter the pit.

"You need to know what it feels like to wrestle one of these bad boys," Catori continued, looking around the moat to make sure no alligator was sneaking up on him. "I'll pick a small one and tape up its mouth with electrical tape. You can get on its back. That's how we train new wrestlers."

"I don't know," I again replied, but the tone of my voice was changing. He was slowly talking me into it.

Catori knew it, too, and he looked me square in the eyes. "Your uncle knew what it was like to be one with an alligator. Admit that you want that same feeling, too."

I thought for a second. Catori was right. I did want that feeling. Nervously, I nodded to the moat. "Tape one up," I said as I kicked off my shoes. "And, Catori…"

"Yeah?"

"Make sure it's one with a smooth back."

Catori and I walked back towards the parking lot. Sweat poured down my face, chest and arms in thick, sticky streams. Sand covered my legs. I had a feeling of total exhaustion and absolute exhilaration all at the same time. "That was fucking incredible, my friend." I exhaled forcefully. I still could barely catch my breath and my heart was pounding. "I can't believe I just got in a pit with an alligator."

"Do you want to go back and do it again?" Catori asked pointing his thumb back over his shoulder. "I'll get one without tape."

I laughed out loud at the young man's suggestion. "No, thanks," I replied. "I just became one with an alligator. The next time, one of my parts could become a part of him. I think I'll just live with the memory."

Catori was putting his shirt back on as we walked. I again noticed the scratch scars on both arms. "Tell me how you feel," he asked.

I wiped the sweat back through my hair and tried to focus my thoughts. "The eyes," I replied. "I'll definitely remember his eyes."

"What about the eyes?" my new life instructor quizzed.

"Dark," I replied as I thought it through. "All-knowing, but evil. What Satan's eyes would look like."

Catori pointed to my leg. "He got you," he said.

I looked down and saw the blood trickling from a scratch the alligator had given me on my calf. "So he did," I replied. "How about you?" I pointed to his arms. "It looks like you've been scratched a few times, too."

Catori shook his head. "I've never been chomped or scratched too badly," he replied. He flexed his arm. "These scars are from tribal tradition – given to me during the Green Corn Festival."

"Kind of like a tribal tattoo," I replied.

"Yeah," Catori said. "Something like that." His tone indicated he did not expect me to understand the tradition.

"That's very cool," I responded. I touched the scars on his left arm. "It certainly makes you unique in this place."

Catori smiled. "The uncle you speak of …"

"Yeah?"

"He would be proud of you today – very proud of you."

The comment caught me off guard and I froze in my tracks. Memories of my uncle flashed through my mind in a split second. Quite unexpectedly, tears welled up in my eyes. "Thanks," I stammered. The comment had taken my breath away and I was unable to respond or move. I searched for something else to say, but all I could do was simply repeat myself. "Thanks."

I got to the exit of the park and said my goodbyes to Catori. I grasped his hand and looked into his eyes. "You're a good man, Catori," I said. "It's truly been a pleasure."

As I started to walk to my car, I heard Catori call my name. When I turned, he was walking in my direction. "Yeah?" I asked.

Catori pursed his lips and nodded thoughtfully. "I think that I might know someone who can help you." He explained to me that he knew an old Seminole who used to live on one of the reservations back in the 70s and offered to talk to him on my behalf. Catori gave me complicated directions to a desolate road in the middle of the swamp, explaining that it contained a bar frequented by the older Seminoles in his tribe. He agreed to talk to the man he knew to see if he could assist in my quest to find some vestige of my uncle. "He's old though and reaching the end of his days on earth," Catori said. "He can't always travel even the short distance it takes to get to this place. He's very sick."

"I understand," I replied, sincerely touched by Catori's continued assistance.

"Go to that bar tomorrow at noon," Catori instructed. "If there is an old orange Ford pickup truck parked out front, go inside. The man I know will approach you."

"And if the truck isn't there," I asked.

"Turn around and go back," Catori warned. "Without him waiting for you, you won't be welcome there."

Chapter Six

Just before I crossed from the mainland to Key Largo, I decided to stop at Alabama Jack's, a little bar about a hundred feet or so north of the tollbooth for the Card Sound Bridge. It was still relatively early and I did not quite feel like eating the full course meal served at the resort. Still, I had skipped lunch and I had not had anything in my belly since breakfast. The drive back following the alligator wrestling left me hungry and thirsty. An ice-cold beer and a big cheeseburger sounded pretty good. Alabama Jack's had the appearance of a bar that would serve both.

Alabama Jack's is open-air on three sides and sits right on a little canal that leads out into Card Sound. From the license plates in the parking lot, it appeared to cater to the diverse kind of clientele that can be found in a good bar in the Keys – a combination of locals, tourists, and bikers. I parked the car, ventured in and confirmed my assumption. A young woman with spiked blue hair and tattoos down her arms sat on a stage strumming an acoustic guitar. Her appearance was at odds with her folk/country tunes, but so it goes in the Keys. She was finishing up an Emmy Lou Harris tune and leading into *Losing My Religion* by REM.

My waitress led me to a table that faced a beautiful mangrove swamp. From my seat on the deck, I could have tossed a line just short of the mangroves and probably caught my own dinner. But when the waitress asked me for an order, I opted for whatever was already in the kitchen. The waitress headed back to the kitchen to deliver my dinner as I listened to the singer.

The people who claim a spiritual experience from listening to *Losing my Religion* probably do not realize the song is about a crush that Michael Stipes had on a man. Nevertheless, the song does strike a chord with people of faith. Everyone can relate to losing their faith from time-to-time. Personally, I have lost and found my relationship with the Lord so many times in my life that my guardian angel needs a scorecard to keep up with my spiritual mood swings. My belief in a higher power and an after-life never wavered. But my delivery system has been all over the board.

As a kid, my family attended a non-denominational Christian church. I grew up with Bible thumping, Hell-fire damnation, gospel hymns, and tent revivals. As a teen, the family switched to the Presbyterian Church, a move that had very little to do with John Calvin and the Scottish Reformation of the 16th Century. The change in religious venue came when we moved to the next town over and the Presbyterian Church was in the same block as our new house. Our pastor would have believed the move was predestined, but dad just wanted to walk to church instead of drive.

In adulthood, I bounced from church to church, searching for religious theology matching my views at each given particular time. In the end, my search led me back to a non-denominational theology and no church to call home. I still believe in God, but I am uncomfortable with any organized group interpreting the Bible for my spiritual well-being.

I am a practicing Christian. I just do not go to the games.

If God is omnipotent, how is it a man interprets His word for me? I'll leave my judgment day to God, rather than some third party in a black robe scaring me into weekly attendance. There is no morality in acting out of fear.

If I believed in my heart the religious dictates of my youth, Gator would be in Hell. By anyone's account, he did things that were outside the bounds of all religious mores. To look at those actions under the microscope of the Ten Commandments, however, would be to ignore that, taken as a whole, Gator was a moral man. Sure, his compass varied from most of society. Back then Gator was a louse. By today's standards he would be labeled as a Renaissance Man. If true, then morality becomes a standard that changes with the times rather than an unchanging law. I refuse to believe that Gator is not waiting for me in the hereafter. I'll not leave judgment to the religious flock that decry homosexuals to Hell and then get their sins washed away by clutching beads and chanting.

I should have requested a song to follow up *Losing My Religion*. "Before you accuse me, take a look at yourself" would be an appropriate opening line. I was well into my meal when the young lady on the stage walked past me. "You have a nice voice," I complimented.

"Thanks," she stopped at my table as she replied and brushed back her blue mane.

"Your Emmy Lou song would have made Emmy Lou proud," I smiled. Better Emmy Lou than telling her she sounded like Michael Stipes.

"That's really sweet," she said.

"And I didn't expect you to be a folkie," I said. I took a drink from my beer before continuing. "No disrespect, but you really don't look the part."

"Looks can be deceiving," she laughed.

"I'll say," I said. "How did you get into this style of music?"

"My dad was a folkie," she said, getting a distant look in her eye as she spoke. I struck a nerve. "He used to play in a trio in the Village in New York. They were pretty popular at the time. He taught me to play guitar when I was just a kid and I grew up learning all the old folk classics. We'd play together every night until it was my bedtime and then he'd head to the Village for his gig."

"So you became a folk performer?"

"Well, not at first," she laughed and shook her head. "I had an all-girl, head-banger band and we'd play some pretty heavy metal. Then I dropped the band and followed a girl down here to Florida. We split up and I started looking for work. All the bars were looking for acoustic players. I'm not one to suffer for my music, so I pawned my Fender, picked up a used Martin and started playing stuff my dad taught me. That was five years ago and I'm still in the Keys." She pointed her thumb over her shoulder back at the stage. "And, I'm still playing folk."

"Back to your roots," I smiled.

"Yeah, I guess," she said. She nodded her head towards the stage. "Hey, I'd love to stay here and talk music, but I gotta get back to work. Got anything you want to hear?"

I thought for a minute. "Here's some folk roots for ya. How about playing *Long Black Veil*?"

"I do that one," she replied, "but I generally do it with my partner. He's off tonight. So, unless you play …"

She seemed to be asking, so I jumped in. "I've got my uncle's 1948 Gibson Flattop in the trunk."

"You got an old Gibson Flattop?"

"Yeah," I knew that would get her attention. I did not play real well, but I was feeling cocky after my Everglades trip. "I can knock down C – D – G with the best of 'em."

"E minor?" she asked with a grin, strumming an air guitar as she spoke.

"My favorite chord," I laughed. Damn. I laughed. It was not a gut buster, but it was genuine. I had not remembered laughing like that in a long time.

"Go get it," she instructed and a few minutes later I was standing on stage tuning up Gator's old Gibson Flattop. The sun was about an hour from falling off the western horizon and beautiful shards of white light were dancing across the dark blue bay. Ever since Gator taught me to play, I kept up with it, but never played much in public. Suddenly, it felt natural. He was channeling through my fingers to the frets on the old beat up guitar. Normally very self-conscious of my playing ability, I was ready to perform.

"I'd like to bring up an old dear friend of mine ..." The woman looked at me quizzically.

"James," I paused. It sounded too formal. Folk singers are not named James. "Jimmy Conrad."

"Jimmy Conrad," she shook her head at the awkward introduction. "And a song we'd like to play for you now," her eyes got a little misty as she struggled with the next words, "one of my dad's favorites ... *Long Black Veil*. Jimmy you take the lead."

A few people applauded as I began to strum out a G chord and leaned into the microphone.

> *Ten years ago,*
> *On a cold dark night,*
> *Some one was killed,*
> *Neath the town hall lights.*
> *There were few at the scene,*
> *But they all did agree,*
> *That the boy who ran,*
> *Looked a lot like me.*

We sang with such joy and enthusiasm that the chorus seemed to flow naturally from our lips. When we finished the song, the crowd applauded. We both laughed and complimented each other about how good we sounded together. She said she only had a couple of tunes left in the set and invited me to sit in. I was not about to leave the stage. I tried to provide her a decent rhythm and followed her changes as best I could. I even offered a bit of harmony as she sang.

My mood was light-hearted as I drove back to the resort. Because it's all open air, Alabama Jack's closes before dark. After the sun goes down, the mosquitoes from the swamp get too thick to stay open into the evening. I had a good buzz going from playing with the girl and I did not want it to end. The thought of possibly meeting with the old Seminole man heightened my mood even more. I pulled into the resort and, after a quick shower, I headed straight to the bar with a definite swagger in my step.

"Well, mon, look what the cat dragged in," Everton laughed as I approached the bar. The sun had gone down and the barflies were starting to fill the pool deck. His station was empty. "Did you find Alligator Alley okay?"

"Wasn't a problem," I confirmed. I pulled out a cigarette and Everton offered a light. "Your directions were great."

He looked at his watch. "You're just getting back, though."

"Yeah," I smiled. "I made a couple of stops along the way."

"Looks like the last one involved a little extra lubricant," Everton noticed.

"It did," I said. "I stopped down at Alabama Jack's."

"Cheating with another bartender, mon," he joked. "I'm jealous."

"Not to worry, Everton." I leaned up to the bar. "I'm yours for the night. Do with me as you like. And, by the way, I'd like to keep the buzz going. Give me another dark rum and anything. In fact, make it a double."

"Put it on my tab, Everton," came a sultry voice from behind me. I turned. It was Lilith approaching the bar. "Back for another touch-and-go?"

"No." The night before, I had looked at Lilith's body as we spoke. Tonight, as she offered to pay for my drink, I looked into her eyes instead. They were blue and inviting. "I've been on the road all day. I'm a little thirsty."

"Good," she replied, nodding at Everton to serve her regular drink. "I'd like to have someone to drink with to-night."

"I find it hard to believe you have trouble finding some-one to drink with." There was a snide tone to my comment. I tried to stop it, but it just came out

"And what's that supposed to mean?" She looked disappointed at my comment rather than angry.

Lilith's gaze embarrassed me. I had just passed on her the same kind of judgment I had so often condemned when coming from others. It was not like me and I was upset with myself. "I'm sorry."

"That didn't come out right. Let's start over," I said.

Once we started to talk, it turned out that we had more in common than I had anticipated. Lilith had a husband much like my wife, high earning and driven. He was on the road as much as my wife. Lilith was prone to finding her salvation in the bottom of an Everton Santiago cocktail glass. The woman I had taken to be "easy" was more complex than I first thought. I told her my story and she was truly empathetic. She understood my marital frustration far too well.

After a couple rounds of drinks, I suggested we take a walk. In silent reply, she stood and nonchalantly tossed a silk scarf onto her barstool as a place marker. Everton nodded as she walked away, knowing not to let anyone sit in her spot.

For the first time, I noticed Lilith was slightly taller than me. She led the way as her dishwater blond hair fell gently down her well-tanned back. I was nervous contemplating how this might proceed. The half-moon cast a pale light that reflected off the water onto the catamarans run ashore on the beach. We were just out of the sight of the bars, but the sounds of the nightly revelers echoed through the air. The breeze off the Atlantic was cool and I could smell Lilith's sweet perfume. She sat down on the edge of one of the catamarans and crossed her toned legs. I walked just past the boats and leaned back against a retaining wall next to her. I tried unsuccessfully to steady my breathing. She laughed at my attempt to try to look cool. When I realized what she was laughing about, I laughed as well. My nerves lightened up a bit.

"So," I smiled. "You seem to be a regular here."

"I come down a lot," she replied as she sipped the drink she had carried down with her.

"Why?" I asked. She cocked her head. It was not a question she had expected. She started to stammer out a response, but I cut her off. "It's probably none of my business," I said.

Lilith smiled. "It isn't," she replied, but her eyes looked as if she actually wanted to explain.

"Then why do you come here every night?" I asked. "Is it the thrill of the hunt?"

She tilted her head to the other side, thinking about the question. "That's certainly an interesting way to put it." She looked at me with knowing eyes that made me blush. "Does it really matter right now?"

"Maybe," I replied. "It's just that you're pretty and intelligent. You don't need to be doing this."

"I love my husband," she replied. "I just don't know that I like him anymore. I come down here to find people I like. You're not game I'm stalking. You're someone I like. I need physical interaction right now with someone I like."

I understood all too well. "Come here," I instructed.

"Why?" Lilith asked slyly.

"Because I want to kiss you."

Lilith put the drink down and slowly walked to me. We kissed, tentatively at first. After a second kiss, she leaned back. "I sure didn't expect this tonight. I thought I scared you off last night."

Rather than answering, I spun Lilith around and pinned her against the wall. I kissed her again. Hard. Passionately. She was taken off-guard, but opened herself to my advance. She ran her fingers seductively through my hair as we kissed.

When we finished the kiss, Lilith pulled back and turned down the top of her sundress. She was not wearing a bra and her breasts stood straight out revealing a well-done boob job. I lowered my lips to her dark, erect nipples. Lilith pushed me back and started to unbutton my shirt. Once she had undone a few buttons, she ripped the rest of them open in one quick pull. She ran her hands inside my shirt, then up and down my sides. I was enjoying her caress when she leaned down and bit my nipple. It surprised me a bit and I yelled out. Lilith laughed as she pulled me close – our exposed torsos pressed hard against each other and we kissed again. This time we savored the kiss. Her hard nipples pressing against my chest was causing a quick and obvious response.

I ran my hands up under Lilith's dress and along her ass to discover she was not wearing any underwear. I hesitated. Her skin was smooth and tight. I could tell that she worked out and felt slightly self-conscience at the poor state of my own body. Lilith did not seem to care as she roughly tugged at my belt. Together we shoved my pants to my ankles. As music and crowd noise infiltrated the beach from the bar area, we tore at each other with passionate abandon. A sheen of sweat covered our bodies as we rose and fell in rhythm with the surf hitting the beach. I had not felt this kind of sexual fervor in a long time.

Afterwards, we slowly walked back to the bar, each smoking a cigarette. Lilith was carrying her sandals in her other hand. "That was good for a starter," she declared.

"The night's still young," I replied. My shirt was hanging open from the buttons that had gone flying. "What do you have in mind? Do you want to go back to the bar?"

"No. Give me your room key," Lilith demanded. I reached into my sandy pants pocket and handed my key to her. She looked at the room number and headed for the hotel. "Go tell Everton to send up champagne and straw-berries."

"Yeah?"

"Yeah," Lilith encouraged. "And get my scarf. You'll like what we do with it when you get there."

Chapter Seven

"You did what?" Catori's father, Micco, an elderly man with long flowing gray hair was not pleased with what his son had just told him and the pitch in his voice rose as he spoke. Micco stifled a cough with his hand.

"He seemed to be a good man, Father," Cattori said. He squared his chin in an effort to hold his ground. "He treated me with respect."

Catori knew that Micco was old-school Seminole and he did not trust outsiders. He understood from the start of the conversation that convincing Micco to break bread with James Conrad would be a hard sell. True to form, the revelation his son had offered for him to meet with some white man the next day had annoyed Micco. His leathery old skin wrinkled on his forehead more than usual.

Catori could see the blood pressure in the old man start to rise. His father had not been in the best of health recently and he regretted riling him up so badly. "Calm down, Father," Catori instructed as he sat down next to his father. He patted Micco gently on his knee. "Have you been taking your heart medicine?"

Micco looked away. "It makes me too shaky," he snarled.

"But the medicine keeps you alive," Catori replied.

"The Master of Breath keeps me alive, my son," Micco

said as he politely removed his son's hand from his knee. "I do not place my eternal soul in the hands of some wasichu doctor."

"Our doctor isn't wasichu," Catori insisted.

"Went to some fancy medical school in New York to learn his medicine," Micco replied. "His skin may be the same as ours, but his ways are that of wasichu. I'd rather be tended to by a shaman and his bundles than have some pills shoved down my throat twice a day."

Catori looked to his mother, Onida, in a desperate, silent plea for support. She made eye contact with her son but shook her head indicating that her involvement would be of no benefit. Micco could be stubborn when it came to just about everything in his life regarding the Seminole way. A doctor-ordered, twice daily dose of heart medicine was no exception.

"I spent yesterday sitting in the chickee." Micco looked at his son bravely, his dark eyes revealing a canvas of knowledge. "I heard the huppe call my name."

Catori ignored his father's reference to an owl calling his name in death. Micco always used Seminole references around him in defiance of being pulled against his will into the twenty-first century. Catori assumed this was just another one of his father's flowery Seminole tribal allusions.

Catori looked to Onida for a reaction. Realizing the comment had been largely ignored, Micco hung his head and sighed heavily.

Onida tried to bridge the divide between her husband and son. "Micco, it's not like Catori told this man where we live. This James Conrad knows nothing of you. If you don't want to go tomorrow, we'll just stay home."

"But you should go," Catori insisted. "I felt trust in this man, Father, and you should trust my judgment."

"I do trust you, son," Micco explained. "I just do not trust wasichu."

Catori looked at his father. "You trusted Holita."

*   *   *

Micco stood tall and reverent before the nine members of the tribal council representing the various reservations within the State of Florida. Micco was one of the youngest people in the room. The six men and three women were all dressed in various colorful patchwork jackets and dresses, although Micco noticed that two of the men wore white shirts and neckties below their traditional garb. A picture of the famed Seminole leader Billy "Osceola" Powell hung on the wall behind the council. The audience was packed tight with elders from the various reservations and the room was hot and sticky. A fan in the doorway did little more than exchange the hot air from the outside with the hot air inside.

Up for discussion was an issue of grave importance to them all – whether they should sell tribal land to the United States government so Alligator Alley could be completed across the heart of the Everglades from Naples to Ft. Lauderdale. It was a discussion that caused great controversy in the Seminole Nation, as well as amongst the East Coast, white business establishment. People from Ft. Lauderdale wanted the road, while those from Miami generally preferred travelers continue to use the old Tamiami Trail.

"When our forefathers were pushed back into the swamp by the government," Micco said as he spread his arms, "this is where we stood our ground." Micco was wearing a turquoise blue and red long shirt that was hand-made for him by his mother, Tayanita, with the bright and colorful patchwork of the Koo-we Clan. The pose he struck with his arms outspread was of bold pride. "And now you propose to sell it to the people who pushed us here in order that they might build a road across our sacred ground."

"Micco," pleaded one of the men wearing a tie under his jacket, "you are so very young and filled with too much emotion. The Seminole Wars have been over for a long time."

"Yes," Micco replied. "And for over 100 years this is where we have made our home." Several of the older men in the audience nodded their heads in agreement as Micco spoke. "They took all but this from us," he continued. "It is where our people made their stand. This ground that you propose to sell is sacred."

"It's nearly 1970," the man sitting at the head of the table offered. "Micco, times are changing. We need to become more self-sufficient as a people."

Micco was quick to reply. "By our very nature," he said, "we are a self-sufficient people. The white men with whom you desire to do business made us self-sufficient."

"Completion of this road can bring us much needed commercial development." One of the other men at the table cut right to the heart of the matter.

"What?" interjected Micco. "Now money matters more than our culture?"

"Culture," boomed the man at the head of the table with a sneer. "What do you know of our culture? You are learning it from a wasichu."

Micco's back went stiff and he balled up his fist. Everyone in the tribe knew of the young man's quick temper. His initial instinct was to leap forward and strike the man who had just insulted him. In fact, he started to take a step forward. Yet, he knew a violent outburst would be counterproductive to his point and show disrespect to an elder. He would lose the support of those who agreed with him. Micco recomposed himself and continued. "When my true father died, it was left to my grieving mother to raise me alone. Holita stepped in and raised me as if I were his own."

The older men in the crowd nodded, remembering how Micco's father had been killed in Korea. They also remember how well Holita had treated Micco and his mother. The older men in the tribe liked and trusted Holita. The attempt to get Micco to blow his cool had failed. Micco hoped the crowd was becoming sympathetic to his arguments. "Holita has proven himself to be just as much a part of this tribe as any of us here tonight."

"But he is not our blood," the tribal leader replied.

"No," said Micco. "Holita is not my – our – blood, but he has insisted I know the ways of our people. The newspapers are already filled with stories of people who want to drain the swamp to build subdivisions. Some are even suggesting there be an airport at the midway point. Our heritage will be lost if this road is built on our land."

"But our heritage is being lost because there is no road, Micco," the leader pressed his case. "Young people like yourself leave the reservation for school or better opportunities and never come back."

"And you think a strip of blacktop through a swamp is going to change that?" Micco replied in mock astonishment.

"Micco," said one of the women in a soft voice. "You are starting to sound like a Dade County Commissioner." The crowd laughed at the reference to the elected officials from Miami fighting the construction of the road in order to protect their own commercial roadway that sent most people from west to east in Florida via the Tamiami Trail.

The snickers that resonated through the room as a result of the insult were the final straw for Micco. "At least I am not the one wearing a shirt and tie like a wasichu politician," he shot back. The leaders may have insulted him, but it could not be a two-way street. When the elders in the crowd gasped, Micco knew he had crossed the line.

"You may attack me and my father, but we care more for this tribe than those of you are already counting the profit you seek." Micco could feel his blood pressure rise. "Go ahead and make a deal with the men who pushed us here in the first place. I hope you get more than a few shiny trinkets and some beads for our ancestor's blood." Micco turned and stormed from the building. When he got to the parking lot, his rage was evident.

Holita was there leaning up against his orange Ford F100 pickup truck and smoking a cigarette. He looked up through his thick glasses. "It looks like it didn't go so well in there," he said.

Micco paced back and forth staring at the ground as he tried to cool down. "It could have gone better," he replied. Micco stopped pacing and looked directly at Holita, who had a look of amusement on his face.

"Then I'd sure hate to see you when things go really bad," said Holita as he started laughing. Micco realized the humor of the situation and also began to smile. "Come on," Holita said. "Let's go back to the boat. You can help me pack for my trip up north."

Micco walked around the front of the truck and jumped into the passenger seat. The truck crunched its way along the shell gravel road and the two remained silent for a long time. Holita taught his adopted son the importance of thoughtful silence, so the pair remained quiet for about half the ride back to their home.

Micco broke the silence. "Let me come with you on this trip," he said.

"I don't think so," Holita replied, looking straight ahead as he drove.

"Why?" asked Micco, "Are you ashamed of me?"

Holita was stunned by the question and pulled the truck to the side of the road. He looked directly at Micco, who was now staring down at the truck's floorboard. "No, son," he replied. "I could never be more proud of someone than I am of you. It took great courage to walk into that room tonight and speak your mind to a group of tribal elders. I could not be more proud of you if you were my own flesh and blood."

"Then let me go north with you this time," Micco insisted.

"No."

"Why?" Micco was nothing if not stubborn.

"Son, it's not you I am ashamed of," Holita said. "It's me."

Micco was confused. "You, Father?" he asked.

"Yes," Holita repeated. "I am ashamed of myself."

"I don't understand," a confused Micco replied.

"Up north," Holita said, "I am a different person. I once had a different life there. Up there, I've done things I'm not proud of. I chose my life, but, behind me, I left some other people's lives in shambles."

"But I'd like to meet your family," Micco insisted.

"I'm not so sure they'd like to meet you," Holita replied. "Most of them never understood why I moved down here to the reservation. I suspect they never will. Maybe the ones that care for me will come to visit someday. You can meet them then."

"You have always been so proud of your nephew," Micco said.

"He's a good boy," Holita laughed. "He wants to be like me, you know."

"So you've said." Micco had heard this story before.

"But he can't," Holita sighed.

"Why not?"

"Destiny."

Chapter Eight

Right now, I would gladly trade my new plasma television for simple peace of mind and a night in bed where my own screams do not wake me from my sleep.

Call my desire for personal serenity a longing for a second shot at so many things – Life 2.0, I guess.

I spent most of my time on earth believing that life was a zero sum game – a personal philosophy based on a fundamental principle that you get out of life precisely what you put into it. I grew up being told those who put in enough hard work would reap an equal amount of success. Wait for success to come to you and you die waiting. Emotionally, it all balances out. Moments of occasional sadness are balanced by laughter. Start feeling too giddy and that feeling of emotional weight starts building right behind the eyes. It all washes out. Zero sum.

Such a core belief in equality rested in an underlying broad world-view that life is fair. I grew up in a small town where I was taught a person's actions lead to parity. My parents, my Sunday school teacher, my girlfriend's mom all told me to work hard and I would succeed. I did not see then what is so clear to me now. They were all feeding me a line of bullshit. Monetary rewards and the material satisfaction that follows may come from hard work, but at some point a person desires more than the newest electronic toy.

My middle-aged malaise likely came from the definition of success adopted by me and my generation. Material wealth was how we measured our own value. Our parents regaled us with stories of how they sacrificed during the depression, wearing their impoverished upbringing as a badge of honor. When our fathers gathered to talk in the alley, it was a competition about who was poorer as a child. They wanted something more for their children, they told us.

We took their suggestion of "something more" and pushed forward with gusto. Our parents were poor and seemingly happy. Possession of things should make us that much happier. We bought the newest car, the largest home and had more nips and tucks to our bodies than any generation before us. Hard work was one way to attain the material success we were led to believe is the measure of one's life.

Unfortunately for us, we never looked at the balance sheet. All the things had credit attached to them. We became a generation of new cars, plasma televisions, McMansions and no money for retirement. So we took on second jobs and tried to convince our egos that down-sizing was not the equivalent of failure. We worked so hard to find a way out and our reward was early heart disease, high blood pressure, and depression.

As I got older, I came to discover that life is not fair. Fairness is at the bottom of the list when it comes to God's cosmic ranking of intrinsic worth. Often those who put the least into living are those who least deserve the rewards a virtuous life bestows, but who somehow get those rewards anyway. One only need watch the nightly news and see the film of who wins the lottery to understand. There was a time when one of the distinctions between the big urban cesspools known as American cities and small communities like the one I grew up in was the way people in the little nooks and crannies of the country took care of each other.

In my town, there was an old guy named Dan who was mentally disabled. His parents were dead and his sister looked out for him. Every day – in a suit and tie – he walked from store to store, checking the wall clocks against his own Timex wristwatch and tearing down the day-to-day calendar that hung behind each cash register. We called him Dan "the Time Man." In the afternoons, Dan would hand-deliver packages from those same shops to their customers for tips and an occasional glass of lemonade or a bologna sandwich. No one ever thought twice about it. Dan was simply doing his job and he did it nearly everyday until the day he died.

I had not thought of Dan in years until last month when we had a going away party at a local bar for several employees who had fallen victim to my company's latest reduction-in-force, an action somehow "demanded" by the dictates of nameless shareholders. As I looked into the eyes of my departing colleagues, I saw the fear in their eyes. Men and women who had dedicated their lives to the success of the company were being cast aside by the demands of capitalism. Then I noticed that the rest of us – those staying at the company – had nearly the same look. Dan "the Time Man" should have taught me a lesson. People are capable of loyalty. Institutions are emotionless bastards.

Shortly after my final visit with Gator, I got my first job as a soda jerk at Pete's. I would take telephone lunch orders for Pete to prepare and then serve up ice cream for malts, sundaes, and cones for all the walk-in customers. I made enough money to occasionally take a girl to the movies and drop a couple of gallons of gas into my old man's car. Flood waters threatened the main drag one year, and I became a hero to all my friends for giving away Pete's ice cream for free before we battened down the store. On Friday nights, Pete let me and a couple of other kids unplug the jukebox and play Dylan tunes, occasionally struggling through Peter, Paul and Mary style harmonies.

My parents brought the whole family to Pete's on my first day of work. Angel was so proud of my strong work ethic. I served my family banana splits and cherry phosphates. The tip Angel left me was as big as the tab itself. I gave it to a kid in my class that bussed tables and washed the dishes. His parents had never been to Pete's to see him work.

The meek may inherit the earth, but it is the assholes who own it during our lifetimes.

I had not woken up with a woman other than Victoria since our wedding day. I was fairly sure that my wife, Victoria, could not say the same thing. Either for that reason, or my own lack of caring anymore, I felt remarkably little guilt. Lilith had been phenomenal in bed, but when I saw her in the light of morning, she had a rugged look to her. Her trip to my bed was not her first time at the rodeo. We spoke little as she left. While I had readied for my trip back to the 'Glades, there was an uncomfortable silence. I did not know whether to thank her for sharing an enjoyable night of sex or apologize for using her for the same.

I kissed Lilith and thanked her. Maybe I was not such an asshole after all.

Blue sky lay ahead in the distance, but the first part of my journey would be through a morning rainstorm. As my windshield wiper slapped back and forth like a metronome, I tried to match a song to the beat. Garden Party by Ricky Nelson came to mind and I began to sing it out loud. The beat was off by just a hair, but I improvised as the wipers pushed water to the side of the windshield with rhythmic regularity. I wanted to call the streams of water tears of a generation, but that seemed a bit too cliché. Still, it fit my mood.

The drive to the 'Glades seemed to take forever. The air did not seem quite as crisp. My eagerness caused me to focus on the odometer, anticipating the click of each additional mile like a child awaiting Christmas morning with the knowledge there were wrapped presents for him under the tree. I fiddled with the radio, trying to find some interesting talk radio show with a topic to take my mind off the present I hoped awaited me.

I got off the north–south road and started onto the road that cut east-west. When I came to the appointed turn, I started following the young Seminole's directions with what I thought was absolute precision. I turned onto an old road that was a combination of gravel and broken shells – good enough to drive on, but not too fast. Thirty minutes later, the road emptied me back onto a main thoroughfare. I pulled to the side of the road and hit the steering wheel in frustration that Catori had given me bad directions.

I snorted and thought for a second. Or, had he. Perhaps the directions were a test. Maybe, in order to find the bar, I had to try a little harder. I turned around and headed back the same road, punishing the rental car at nearly 25 miles per hour as I went. About five minutes into my retraced path, I noticed a small opening to my right. I started to turn my car into the opening in the brush. I questioned my sanity as I drove along the dirt mound, barely a foot or more above the level of the swamp water on either side.

About four hundred yards down the "road," stuck aside a weeping willow, sat a cement brick building with a rusty pole holding a metal sign that simply read: "Bar." Denying my better judgment, I pulled into a parking space. The third car from the front door was an old, beat up, orange Ford pickup truck. I sighed in relief that I had not missed the man. I got out of my car and walked up to the door. A burned out neon Miller Light beer sign was in the front window and a set of alligator head wind chimes hung to the right side of the door frame. It took all my courage to open the door.

The door swung open much harder that I had expected and made a loud noise as it crashed against the inside wall and light shot across the floor. As my eyes adjusted to the light, it was similar to the inside of Duke's Rock Bar that I remembered from my childhood. The old men playing cards were replaced by similar aged guys playing dominos. A dusty pool table with faded and torn green felt sat in the middle of the room.

But thanks in large part to my noisy entrance, the friendly confines of Duke's Rock Bar had been replaced by cold, staring eyes. I quickly realized that I was an unwelcome outsider. Nevertheless, I stepped up to the bar and ordered a draft beer. The bartender made no effort to pour it for me, seemingly insulted that I had even requested service. I repeated my order.

Thoughts of this having been a horrendously bad idea shot through my mind. Just as I was about to turn and leave, a short and stocky Seminole with gray hair approached. He cocked his head and stared intently at me, sizing me up from head to toe. The old man looked at the bartender and said, "Make that two."

The old man had an odd look to him. He was dressed in blue jeans and, despite the warm weather, a flannel shirt with the sleeves rolled up. I looked down and he was wearing a relatively new pair of white Nike cross-trainers. His gray hair was pulled back in a braided ponytail. The bartender nodded at the old man and began to pour two draft beers. As he did, I turned to the old man and stuck out my hand. "Hi," I said. "I'm James Conrad."

The old man said nothing and made no effort to return my handshake. He simply grabbed the two beers and walked back to his table. I followed him to a table in the corner of the bar where a woman was already sitting. When we sat down, he introduced himself. "I am Micco." He nodded to the woman. "This is my wife, Onida."

Onida was a short moon-faced woman. Her skin was a darker hue than Micco's and her pitch-black hair with streaks of grey was pulled back in a ponytail with colorful peyote beads woven into the braids.

"My pleasure," I said, reaching for my beer. I took a sip as the old man eyed me with a combination of curiosity and distrust.

Once he had properly sized me up, he spoke. "My son, Catori, tells me that you are here in the Everglades looking for the memory of someone?"

"Yes," I responded. "Catori said that you might be of assistance."

"He tells me that this man was your uncle."

"Yes," I replied. "My uncle, well my great uncle actually, used to live out here in the 'Glades with a group of Seminoles."

Micco nodded his head in skeptical acceptance of my premise. "Tell me about him," he instructed.

"My uncle was a good man," I started, but then paused, "… misunderstood by many in my family, but a kind and gentle man with a big heart."

"I've known a lot of men claiming to be misunderstood by their families," Micco replied. He did not smile in recognition of his own comment, but remained stoic. "You'll have to be a bit more specific."

"Sure," I chuckled. This old guy was going to be a tough nut to crack. "He was from a small town in Kentucky. He moved to Florida after he got divorced from my aunt. He bought a houseboat and docked it at a tourist stop somewhere out here in the swamp."

"There were a lot of those places off the road back in those days." Micco's tone had changed. He suddenly seemed interested in the story. "This uncle of yours, what did he look like?"

"He had kind of a funny look to him. He was a small guy but had very muscular arms and forearms. He wore big, black glasses that had lenses about this thick." I gestured with my thumb and index finger. "He always wore an African-style pith helmet when he fished."

"And, he liked to fish?" Micco leaned forward.

"Liked?" I replied with a short laugh. "Hell, fishing was his life. He loved to hunt and fish, and could play about any string instrument you put in front of him."

"What was his name?"

"Albert," I replied. "Albert Clarke."

Micco smiled. "Holita," he said in a near whisper.

"Holita?" I asked.

"Holita is a play on 'halputta,' the Seminole word for Alligator," Micco replied.

A huge smile spread across my face before reaching in my pocket to pull out my cigarettes. "Uncle Gator."

"Yes," Micco said. "I knew the man you called Gator."

"Really?" I was delighted. I offered a cigarette to the pair and they refused. "That's incredible. I can't believe you actually knew my uncle."

"Yes," Micco said. "I knew him well, better than anyone in the tribe. But I am a bit unsure of you, my friend. Holita has been gone for many, many years. Suddenly, you show up here on my reservation and claim to be his nephew. How do I know that you are who you say?"

I lit my cigarette and blew out the first puff. "Please tell me more about your knowledge of my uncle. Maybe I can confirm what you know."

Micco thought for a minute. He shook his head. "No." He was obviously not a trusting man.

I breathed the smoke from my cigarette in slowly. "Then we seem to be at an impasse," I said.

"Yes," Micco responded, his eyes never moving from mine.

I thought for a minute and then scooted my chair closer to the table. "Micco, you claim you knew Gator better than anyone in your tribe."

"Yes," Micco replied. "That is quite true."

"Wait here," I said. I stood up and walked out to the rental car. A bit more gentle with the bar door this time, I slapped it shut behind me. I popped open my trunk and pulled Gator's old Gibson guitar from its case and carried it by the neck back into the bar. I approached the table and placed the old guitar on the table in front of Micco.

Micco pulled the guitar across the table and placed it in his lap. He looked at it longingly as he rubbed his hand up and down the neck. Pausing first, he then looked at me. I nodded to his silent question. "Go ahead," I said. "You can play it."

Micco strummed a couple of chords, then closed his eyes and steadied his breathing. When he opened his eyes he looked thoughtfully at the worn down frets on the neck.

"It's a little out of tune," I said apologetically. "I've only played it once since I landed the other day."

Micco nodded, his eyes still searching the body of the guitar. He ran his hand up and down the neck again, then over the face of the body. Micco closed his eyes, brought the wood to his lips and gently kissed it. Without saying a word, Micco got up, placed the Gibson on the table and walked out of the bar.

I was confused. I looked at Onida. "Did I say something inappropriate?" I asked. She said nothing, her face emotionless.

Suddenly, I was alone and I felt very much aware of my surroundings. I was the only white man in an unfriendly, small bar in the middle of the Everglades – a bar that I had trouble finding – a bar off the radar screen of most humans. My mind raced as I considered this entire trip may have been a mistake. The people in this place could roll me, toss me in the swamp and no one would ever know. The shadows of the bar abruptly felt ominous and it seemed as if everyone in the place was staring at me. The hair was standing up on the back of my neck. I considered getting up and running for the door, but sat frozen in my chair.

The opening of the door and the light flashing across the floor of the bar made me jump. I looked back and could see Micco standing in the doorway. He had something in his hand. My initial instinct warned me that Micco had gone out to his truck to get a gun. I felt cold fear and began to stand.

As the door closed behind Micco and he approached, my eyes readjusted to the changing light. I relaxed as I saw that the object in his hand was certainly not a weapon. Micco walked to my side and placed an old mandolin on the table next to my guitar. I recognized it immediately. It was Gator's.

I looked up at Micco, my eyes revealing the thousands of questions racing through my head.

"So, my brother, tell me what brings you here." Micco finally smiled.

I shook my head, unable to speak. When I did not respond he began to tell me his story. Following the death of Micco's natural father in the Korean War, Gator had taken Micco under his wing and raised him as his own child. Micco concluded his story by re-asking the same question he had posed to me minutes earlier. "Does that answer your questions?"

"Yeah," I lied. The story was only starting to sink in. I was certain I was going to have many other questions once I thought it through.

"I asked you before, why did you come out here in the middle of the swamp?"

"I'm not sure."

"I thought that might be your answer," Micco replied. He looked at me closely. "You have a kind face."

"Thank you," I said. "I've had a lot of things said about my looks before, but that's a new one."

"But you look troubled."

I chuckled and shook my head. Micco could not even begin to imagine how troubled I was at the time.

"You find that funny?" Micco asked.

"No," I said. "It's not funny at all. I've known you for only a few minutes and you can already judge me pretty accurately."

"I do not judge," Micco said. "My judgment will make neither of our sins any less."

"Fair enough," I said as I stared into his dark eyes. "But in answer to your question, I'm not entirely sure why I'm here myself."

Chapter Nine

As Onida drove the old orange pickup truck along the dirt road in the reservation, Micco remained silent. The road was bumpy and the worn out shocks on the old truck bounced him around on the frayed bench of the cab. The drive reminded him of why he rarely left his house anymore. He preferred the solitude of his own chickee to just about anything else on earth. Much had happened during the past twenty-four hours, since his son had told him about the stranger searching for his past. He struggled to process it all in his mind. Micco's life had been filled with ebbs and flows that seemed to rise and fall without any warning. Here he was, aging and ill yet meeting the man he wanted Holita to introduce him to years ago. It must have been a gift from the Master of Breath.

Micco closed his eyes and thought back to a night from his past—the night of Holita's purification.

*   *   *

It was the fourth day of Posketv, the tribal New Year. Micco approached Holita's houseboat in a canoe that he and Holita had hewn from a fallen cypress log. The entire tribe had left their chickees for the sacred area that had been set up in the swamp three days earlier and had left Holita alone on the reservation. Micco could see the old man sitting in a chair at the boat's bow, gripping the railing and looking out over the water. The May sun was setting and the "Everything Growing Moon" was about to rise from the east. Smoke was billowing up from the remote hammock of hardwood trees where Micco spent the last three days following the traditions of his people. Holita had already explained to Micco this would be his last Green Corn Festival and he asked that the tribe pray for his soul. Holita was sick and Micco knew it.

Holita heard Micco board the houseboat. He was weak from the cancer and his attempt to get up from the chair was labored. He had to hold onto the railing to turn and see his son. "What are you doing here?" Gator asked, his brow furrowed in confusion. "Aren't you supposed to be out at the ceremony? Did you forget something?"

"No," Micco replied as he approached. "I didn't forget anything."

"Then what are you here for?"

"You, Chacteka." Micco placed his hand gently on the old man's shoulder. He knew that Holita liked to be referred to by the Seminole word for father. "I'm here for you. The tribal elders want you to join us for tonight's dance."

Tears filled Holita's eyes and his knees buckled. He had lived on the reservation for years, but had never been invited to join the tribe for the Green Corn Festival. Few white men had ever actually seen the ceremony. He was overwhelmed with emotion knowing, on the verge of death, they were willing to accept him into their tribal ritual.

"Come on," Micco said softly. "The time is upon us and we need to get going."

Micco held Holita's arm to steady him as they walked to the canoe. He helped Holita step down into it before he shoved off into the canal and began to push the canoe through the water with a long pole. Holita was too old and sick to help. He sat at the front and watched as the alligators lowered into the water before them.

When Micco's father had been killed in Korea, it came as quite a shock to the tribe. His wife, Tayanita, removed all the painted peyote beads from her braids and did not comb her hair until she was ready to remarry – a Seminole tradition for a widowed spouse. Micco, then known by his childhood name of Knoton, had not yet been given his adult name by the tribe. The boy was lost without his father.

Seeing the sudden void that had occurred in Knoton's life, Holita took the young Seminole under his protective wing, teaching him to hunt and fish. Holita made sure that Knoton went to school, but also insisted he rely on tribal leaders to learn the ways of his people. When Knoton's mother finally combed her hair, she went to Holita. They never formally married, but they had lived as a family ever since.

Micco had always thought of Holita as his father. He knew Holita did not have long to live and was pleased the tribal elders had granted his request to allow Holita this experience before he died.

Tayanita, was standing on the shore to greet her son and Holita as they moved slowly to the small island in the swamp where the Green Corn Festival was being held. Micco jumped into the shallow water and pulled the canoe ashore. He steadied the vessel as his mother helped Holita get out. As Holita stood and stretched, his eyes darted from side to side at the flurry of activity.

The men and women were separated from each other. The men were stomp dancing and chanting. Everyone had spent the day purging and fasting and the women were preparing the feast that would be eaten following the ceremony. A wooden platform a couple of inches off the ground separated the men from the women. A freshly built fire was raging and the smell of burning cypress filled the night air.

One of the elders of the tribe approached the trio. He was dressed in a traditional patchwork long shirt. He stood tall as he spoke. "Holita, my friend, you have lived with us for many, many years."

"Yes, I have," Holita replied. "And I have been honored that you have allowed me to do so."

"You have come to know our ways," the elder continued. "And you have insisted that, as a boy, Micco understand his heritage. For that, we have trusted you as one of our own."

"I, too, have found trust in our relationship."

The elder placed both hands on Holita's shoulders. "But, my brother, your time is near. The Master of Breath, to whom all prayers are offered, will be calling you home soon."

"This is true." Holita solemnly replied. "I do not fear death. I am ready to crossover."

"That is why we have asked you here tonight. Your circle is nearly complete." The elder nodded at Tayanita who turned and walked towards the other women. "We, too, want to make sure you are ready to go to the hill to be with Esaugetu Emissee. Tonight you will participate in our dance. It is time for your purification, your renewal. We will celebrate the sacredness of your life and practice forgiveness."

Holita knew that few white men had ever seen the Green Corn Dance, let alone actually participated in it. He bowed his head in a gesture of respect. "Thank you," he uttered.

"I know you are weak from your illness," the man said as they continued to walk, "but you'll have to stay awake through the night. Do you think you can do that?"

Holita nodded, unsure if he could keep the promise he just made.

"I will help him," Micco interjected.

"Then let's begin," the man instructed.

Micco and Holita joined the other men who were now sitting cross-legged around the wood platform. Black tea, brewed from the leaves of holly bushes, was presented to the men and they began to drink it in excessive amounts. In between, tobacco pipes were passed and smoked. It was not long before Holita had to vomit. He was told the ceremony began with purging and, one-by-one, each man left the circle to throw up. They would return, drink more black tea and purge again.

Holita had sampled the concoction before. Black tea always made him jumpy, but drinking continuously on an empty stomach intensified the sensation. He was old, tired and sick, but the excessive amount of tea he had consumed gave him edgy energy. It seemed to electrify every nerve in his body. He was sweating profusely.

Holita was led to a chickee near the fire. He stripped and a loincloth was placed around his waist. The tribe's shaman appeared and two women instructed Holita to lie down on palms that had been laid on the ground. Holita thought he recognized the shaman, but his face had been blackened by ashes from the fire. He wore a mantle of feathers. The shaman opened a bundle of medicine from a wrapping of deerskin and began a stomp dance around Holita, chanting as he circled the old man.

Reverently, the shaman took an owl's claw and placed four parallel scratches on each of Holita's arms and legs. The scratches were deep and began to bleed. The shaman then poured liquid over the open wounds. It stung, but Holita did not flinch. As the shaman turned and poured some of the same liquid on the fire, the women stood on either side of Holita and brushed his body with heron feathers.

Micco helped Holita off the ground and another man lay down in his place.

"I understand the purging," whispered Holita as they walked. "But what's the scratching all about?"

"The scratches and medicine are used to cleanse your body of its impurities," Micco replied. "Let's go to the platform. The Buffalo Dance is about to begin."

A man Holita recognized from the reservation began singing. Two by two, alternative pairs of men and women began dancing around the platform, swaying from side to side to represent the movement of a buffalo. The women had turtle shells filled with beads wrapped around their legs that rattled while they danced.

When the dance was complete everyone gathered, men and women. Tayanita came and served dinner to Holita.

The moon was high in the sky when the Seminoles began the Green Corn Dance. Micco and Holita sat around the platform enjoying the chanting until the sun came up.

After sunrise, tribal leaders carried water to the fire while others began breaking down the encampment. Micco loaded Holita and his mother into the canoe and the three of them headed back to the houseboat. When they arrived, Micco helped Holita step onto the deck of the houseboat.

"Thank you," Holita said as he hugged Micco and kissed him on the cheek.

Tayanita steadied Holita's arm as they led him to his bed.

"Get some sleep, Father," Micco instructed, proud that his father had participated in the purification ceremony. "We'll go fishing later today."

"I'd like that," Holita replied.

Later that day when Micco returned, Holita had quietly slipped into the arms of the Master of Breath.

Chapter Ten

I kept my car close to the pickup truck as we bounced down the dusty road. Close was actually an understatement. I was riding the truck's bumper. It was not that I was afraid of losing my way. The road was barely wide enough for two cars to pass each other, let alone turn around. Side roads seemed to be miles apart. Dead ahead was my only option.

The road was made of built up shell gravel. It was rough and primitive. The posted speed limit of 25 miles per hour seemed a pipe dream. The emergency lane was a swamp where, from the driver's seat in my car, I could spot fish, turtles, snakes, and alligators through the crystal-clear water. I drove past a sign that seemed silly with its "Low Shoulder" warning. Deer bounded back and forth across the road with wild abandon. If I blew a tire on this rough terrain, I wanted to make sure I could get the attention of the folks ahead of me. We were in the rugged, untamed portion of the Everglades. It was beautiful and exotic, but breaking down on this road could be hazardous to my health. AAA was not going to make a service call out here.

Every so often, we passed a small house built on an acre or so patch of gravel similar in makeup to the roadbed, but about a foot or two higher. The side and back yards of the houses was the swamp. Some of the lots had old construction cement brick homes. One lot had an old air-stream trailer buried in deep weeds. Other lots contained relatively new, smartly constructed homes. Almost all of them had traditional Seminole chickees somewhere in the yard. I could not help but think how much you would have to want to get away from it all to live so far out in the middle of nowhere with prehistoric – looking reptiles as your closest neighbors.

As we got closer to the main road, the houses started to become more frequent – the construction more elaborate and newer. The paved portion of the road was in sight when the pickup truck slowed down and put on its turn signal. The lot we were turning onto was larger than the others. The house on the lot was of a similar size, but the adjacent chickee was much bigger than the ones I had seen on the other lots.

Catori was in the front yard working on the engine of a small airboat. He waved at the truck and then spotted me trailing closely behind. He smiled and nodded a greeting before approaching the pickup truck. He helped his father out of the truck.

Despite Catori's encouragement that we retire to the sanctuary of the air-conditioned house, Micco insisted we sit in his chickee. As we walked, Catori explained the new construction I saw along the road was the result of the money each family was receiving from the casinos. Many families used their funds to build newer homes. Catori built this home for him and his parents, although his father still insisted on spending a great deal of his time in the chickee instead of the house.

We stepped up to the platform, walked to the edge and looked out over the Everglades. "I used to sleep out here," Micco explained, pointing to the pad on the floor behind him. "But, now I'm too old. I have trouble getting up off the floor."

"And he doesn't hear as well as he used to," added

Catori, pointing to his own ears. "He doesn't sense the presence of animals like he used to. I came out here one morning and there was a Burmese Python starting to climb up the post." He pointed to a 12 foot snakeskin tacked along the upper rail of chickee. "Damn interlopers are taking over the 'Glades.'"

"They are no more interlopers than we are," Micco interjected as he made his way to a chair and slowly lowered himself down. "Our people were not indigenous here. We were forced here by the government," he said referring to the series of Seminole Wars where Federal troops forced tribes further and further into the swamp. "The python is just as entitled to this land as us."

"Yeah," Catori said. "But that one felt entitled to you."

Micco swatted the thought away with a wave of his hand.

Catori smiled. He liked it when his father was a bit ornery. "Well, he's one that lost his entitlement. They said there's one up by the bar that is twice as long as that one, maybe twenty-five feet. I'd like to have that skin to match."

Onida approached the chickee carrying a tray of fried flat bread, meat and lemonade. Micco took a piece of bread and placed some shredded meat on the bread, wrapped it and took a bite. I followed suit, not quite sure if I was eating beef, pork or a portion of the python hanging above us.

"My father died when I was a young," Micco said, a far-off look in his eye. "Holita, the Seminole name given to your uncle, was living with the tribe at the time. He showed pity on my mother and me. He took me under his wing and became my surrogate father. He made sure I never wanted for anything."

"He was a giving man," I replied. The meat and bread tasted good, but unique. I began to wonder if I was actually eating the snake.

"He made sure I went to school," Micco said.

"Not all the children on the reservation went to school back then," Catori interjected.

"But along with school," Micco continued, "Holita made sure I understood the ways of my people. I grew up more spiritual than many others in my village because of him."

I thought for a moment about what Micco had just said. In much the same way, Gator had helped me understand the small town in which I had been raised. The time we had spent together helped me understand my own place in society. "I can certainly relate," I said. "Gator was a guiding force in my life as well."

Micco picked up his glass and looked at me. "Your uncle spoke of you often," he said before taking a sip of lemonade. "He had quite a fond place in his heart for you."

I smiled. "And, I for him," I replied, content with the thought.

"He once told me that I was living the life you dreamed of living," Micco said, looking intently at me for a response.

"When I was a boy," I started, "I wanted to come to Florida and spend a summer with my uncle. My mother would not let me. She said she was worried about me being bit by an alligator or a water moccasin or something." I took another bite of the bread before continuing. "I think she was more worried about me becoming too much like him."

"And she perceived that to be a bad thing?" Micco asked.

"Yeah," I laughed. "I guess so."

"But no one owned Holita," Micco replied. "He was his own man – lived a life based upon his own set of rules and answered to no one."

"Those might have been personal traits admired in Seminole culture," I replied. "But where I grew up, it was not in line with the mores taught to me by my parents."

Micco nodded and we both remained silent for awhile contemplating our own unique relationships with my uncle. In a way he had prepared us both for the lives we had come to live.

"I am tired," Micco broke the silence. "And I need to lie down for awhile. But I'd like for you to stay with us for the evening. We will fix a traditional dinner over an open fire."

"I'd be honored," I replied.

Micco stood up, balancing himself on Onida's arm as he stood. "Catori will show you around the Everglades while I sleep. The two of you can catch our dinner," he said and then turned for the house. As they walked, I heard Micco tell his wife to call for the shaman.

"That's a first," Catori said as we watched Micco walk to the house.

"What?" I asked.

"You are the first white man my father has ever asked to stay at our home."

My airboat ride into the Everglades with Catori was far different than the boat ride I had been on the day before. The tourist boat had several rows of seats to accommodate paying customers. Catori's boat was much smaller, obviously built for personal use. Fishing gear was secured against the hull, along with a cross-bow and spear. I felt very self-concious as I helped shove the boat into the water, standing calf deep in the water. I tried not to keep looking down for snakes. I took little comfort from the fact that Catori was barefoot. Every sliver of lilly pad and grass that brushed against my leg felt like the 25 foot python Catori had mentioned earlier.

We zoomed across the saw grass toward a small island grove of cypress trees I could see in the distance. It was far too noisy to make conversation, but Catori would occasionally tap me on the shoulder and point out various animals in the distance – deer, heron and, of course, alligators. We slowed and ran the boat up onto the shore of the small island. Catori put together his crossbow while I tied a spoon lure onto the end of some fishing line. We jumped onto the island and walked quickly and silently to its other side, where a ledge of rocks looked over into about three feet of water. There I saw more species of fish than I could seemingly count. Some I recognized; bass, snook, gar all swam about, but there were many others I did not recognize. Before casting a line, I watched as Catori set a spear into the crossbow. He looked at me and I nodded that he should go first. Catori squared his shoulders and took aim. The spear plunged into the water and right through a 5 pound bass.

Catori pulled the bass to the shore, removed it from the spear and tossed it into a cooler we had carried with us from the boat. "Want to give it a try?" Catori asked.

"Naw," I replied as I tossed my first cast out into the water. "I'd rather wrestle another alligator." A snook hit the lure and immediately started to run.

"Get him, James," Catori encouraged as I adjusted the drag on the line and started to pull the fish towards us. It was not a large fish, but he had a lot of fight in him. "Work him. Work him," Catori continued. He reached for the line as the fish got close. Once I had the fish close to the ledge, Catori grabbed the fish by the lower lip and pulled the lure out. He held it up for me to admire before tossing it into the cooler. It did not take long until we had more than enough fish for dinner.

I sat on the cooler, fish still flipping around inside, and lit up a cigarette. "The water is so damned clear," I said.

Catori was wrapping up his crossbow. "The Everglades is the widest and most shallow river in the world," he said. He pointed north. "It starts up in the lake country and runs down to the Gulf and Keys."

"That's why it's not salty," I responded.

"Right," said Catori. "It's fresh water fed. And, by the time this water has reached us, it's been filtered over a couple hundred miles of saw grass, sand, and rocks. It's not a bog. The 'Glades is one big river constantly flowing south."

I puffed on my cigarette. "It's certainly the most unusual ecosystem I've ever encountered."

"And we've coexisted with nature here for a couple of hundred years," Catori said.

"So what happens in the next hundred?" I asked as I continued to smoke my cigarette.

"I'm not sure," he responded.

"Not sure? Why?" I asked. His response seemed strange.

"Old traditional Seminoles like my father are few and far between," Catori said. "Most of my friends are happy to get their monthly checks from the casino and send their kids to private schools in Miami. The bigger the checks get, the more our people leave the reservation."

"So why are you still here?" I asked.

"My father would never leave this place," Catori replied. "So I took my money and built a house for all three of us that would suit him. That's why I have the elaborate chickee. It's a combination of what he wanted and what I wanted. My father was born here and he'll die here."

When we got back to the house, Micco and Onida were already making preparations for dinner. A traditional Seminole fire was burning between the house and the chickee. Four long cypress logs were pointing in the directions of the compass. The fire where the four logs met was small and there was a pot hanging over the flames. "I've never seen a fire built like that," I said.

"It lasts longer that way," Catori explained. "As the fire goes down, we simply push the logs in more towards the middle."

Micco had overheard the conversation and approached. "White men build big fires and sit far away," Micco smiled. "We build small fires and sit closer."

Micco led us to the chickee and sat down in his chair. Two other chairs had been arranged around a small wood table. Plain white ceramic coffee cups sat empty on the table. As Catori and I climbed onto the platform of the chickee, Micco waved his arms toward the two vacant chairs, inviting us to sit with him.

As Catori sat, he grimaced looking at the coffee cups. "I suppose that you've made us tea for the evening, Father?" he asked.

"Yes," Micco replied. "I know that you do not like black tea, but it is one of our traditions."

"I know," Catori replied. "I should have eaten lighter today." The grimace was still riding his face.

"Black tea?" I asked. Onida stepped onto the platform of the chickee and filled our glasses with steaming clear liquid from a kettle. "What do you mean by black tea? I assume we're not talking Lipton here."

Catori lowered his voice to a whisper as Micco closed his eyes and began to quietly chant, seemingly blessing the tea. "Black tea is a traditional drink of the Seminole," Catori explained. "Not too many people even know the recipe anymore, but it's brewed from holly leaves and loaded with caffeine."

"Energy drink on steroids," I replied as I looked at the cup in front of me.

"And one other thing," Catori added. "It makes you vomit."

"You're kidding me, right?" I asked before realizing the disdain evident in my voice.

Micco stopped chanting and opened his eyes. "Purging yourself is the first step of purification," Micco said softly.

"Purification," I said softly.

"Isn't that what you are here looking for, James?" Micco asked.

"I'm not sure," I stammered. "I haven't been quite able to put my finger on why I'm here."

"You seek a renewal in your life," Micco replied. "You may leave if you like. But out of respect for my father – your uncle – tonight I offer you a chance for renewal. If you agree to the journey, the Maker of Breath will forgive all your past transgressions and you will start anew."

I thought for a moment about my own life and the spirituality I had often sought, and always seemed to lose, over and over again. I reached forward and grabbed the steaming cup.

"Drink it quickly," Micco instructed as he took his cup in hand. "It makes the end result easier."

I drank the black tea down as quickly as I could, and the other two followed suit. Onida refilled our glasses and we chased down a second and then a third cup. It did not take long for me to rush to the side of the chickee. I grabbed a support pole for the thatch roof and began to throw up over the side. My forehead dripped with sweat. I was throwing up so violently that I barely noticed Micco and Catori doing the same thing. Once I had finished, I slowly returned to my seat. I was dismayed when Onida filled my cup again. Apparently, this was going to take awhile.

After several rounds of black tea, my belly was empty and my nerves were on fire. Catori was right when he said this stuff was high in caffeine. I was wired as tightly as I had ever been in my life. The speed I had taken at exam time in college had nothing on this stuff. My heart was pounding so hard that I was concerned it would explode. Sweat poured from every pore in my body. I was quietly relieved when Onida removed the cups from the table.

"The shaman came by while you were out in the water," Micco said. He started to place some items on the table. It was dark now and bugs started to fill the air. Their buzzing seemed heightened by the senses of my own buzz. I looked at Catori as I swatted at a mosquito that appeared to be the size of a small bird.

"Medicine Man." Catori was starting to get used to my inquisitive nature and answered my question before I was even able to ask it. Catori walked off the platform and grabbed several handfuls of myrtle bush leaves. When he came back, he put them in my hands. "Crunch these up and rub them on your arms and legs. It will keep the mosquitoes away."

"The shaman could not stay," Micco continued. "But he left me his bundles for our use." Micco continued to place more items from the bundles on the table.

"Bundles contain our spiritual medicines," Catori continued the narrative for my benefit, while Onida appeared back on the platform of the chickee with a new kettle. I was silently praying it was not more black tea for us to drink. She slowly began to sway and, as she hummed a monotonic tune, step in place. I noticed she had something strapped to her legs that made a clicking noise. They looked like the shells of box turtles.

"Catori," Micco instructed his son. "Give me your arm."

Catori held his arm out steady while Micco took something in his hand that made deep scratches on his wrist. "An owl's claw," Catori said as blood began to flow from his arm. "This is what caused the scars on my arms that you saw the other day."

Micco looked at me. "James," he said as he held out his hand for me to join them.

My own eyes were fixed on Catori's bleeding arm. The combination of Onida's ritualistic low humming and my system in caffeine overdrive was making the entire scene seem surreal.

"James," Catori said sternly in order to get my attention.

My eyes snapped to Catori's. "What?"

"Give Father your arm," Catori instructed.

I was wound as tight as a jacked-up speed addict and my leg nervously twitched up and down on the platform as I considered my next move.

"James," Micco said softly. "Give me your arm."

For some unknown reason, I followed Micco's gentle instruction. I stood up and held my arm out in front of him while he raked the owl's claw across my wrist. The stinging was intensified by the caffeine buzz. He took my arm and fused it against Catori's, who seemed stunned by the action. Catori looked questionably at his father as Onida poured hot liquid over our joined wrists.

Micco looked at Catori. "Now I know why the owl called my name," Micco said before letting go of our arms. He silently turned to walk from the chickee. I started to pull my arm away, but Catori grabbed them and kept them fused. His eyes were filled with tears.

"What?" I asked looking quickly from Micco to Catori. "What just happened?"

"Remember what your uncle told you about being one with the alligator?"

"Yes," I replied.

"You and I, James," Catori said softly. "We are now one."

When I awoke the next day, my buzz was gone, my belly was full and my mind was as confused as ever.

Chapter Eleven

"We're going to go out into the Atlantic and fuck on this little boat," Lilith said, her head slightly cocked, with her right hand on a hip in a pose that was radiating sensuality. "Kinky."

"No," I laughed as I tossed some fishing gear into the port compartment of a rented 21' Ranger Intercoastal fishing boat. As I looked at Lilith out of the corner of my eye, her suggestion of sex at sea did not sound like such a bad idea. She was dressed in black shorts and a low-cut red halter-top that showed her middrift.

After I had returned to the resort from my overnight stay at Catori's house on the reservation, I had slept the day away. The ceremonial black tea and the night's events had kept me up long into the night. After purging, we had eaten until we were stuffed. Catori and I had chanted while Micco and Onida had danced traditional stomp dances. I had slept in Catori's guest room. Actually, sleep is stretching it. The black tea had made my sleep shallow. I had awakened early and made plans with Catori to go fishing again before I headed home. When I got back to the resort, I had Everton pour me two strong drinks and I headed to my room where I slept the afternoon away.

I met Lilith at the bar following dinner. When I told her to go home and return in something more casual, this outfit was not quite what I had expected. I was tempted to skip the whole trip and head back to my room. Lilith brought out some inner sexual depravity in me and she knew it. In fact, I think she liked making me react in a manner I never would in my life back home. There is a fine line between muse and siren.

Still, my hardening dick notwithstanding, I wanted to get out on the water. My day with Micco and his family had been serene and invigorating all at the same time. The ceremony with the scratching had seemed weird, but I felt at peace for the first time in a long time. My head was not filled with worries of meetings on my schedule or reports about my quarterly numbers. That life seemed a lifetime away. I did not want to go to a bar to contemplate the implications of the previous day. Alcohol was not what I needed to understand what was happening to me. I wanted to go fishing. Interestingly, I did not want to go out on the water alone. I knew only two people on the island and one of them, Everton Santiago, was serving drinks at the bar.

"No," I repeated as I reached up and offered Lilith a hand to step from the dock to the boat. "We're going fishing."

Lilith pulled back her hand tentatively. "Fishing?" she asked.

"Yeah." I smiled as I pushed out my open palm a second time.

"Baby," said Lilith, "I haven't been fishing since I was in grade school."

"Then this is a great night to relive your childhood," I said. "The guy I rented this from told me how to get to a couple of his favorite honey holes."

"If we would have stayed at the bar, you could have had my honey hole," Lilith mumbled.

"Come on," I said. "What do you have to lose?"

"My dignity," Lilith mumbled as she moved forward, shaking her head as she stepped onto the boat.

I laughed at Lilith's comments. I started to fire off some wise ass line about how much I had paid to rent the boat for the night, and that a hooker would have been cheaper. I thought better of it and said nothing. Instead, I unhooked the tie rope from a cleat on the dock, pushed off and fired up the engine. Lilith sat down, her crossed arms and legs matching the scowl on her face. One of the places I had been told to fish was not too far from the dock we were leaving, but I determined it best to cruise around awhile to let Lilith calm down. Once I was out of the no-wake zone, I pulled the throttle back and felt the front of the boatlift. I looked over and watched Lilith sink back in her seat. It was faint, but as we picked up speed, I thought I saw the beginnings of a smile.

Personally, I understood her loosening up. I was enjoying the salt spray in my face and I was in no real hurry to wet my line.

The pounding of the hull of the boat against the surf brought back childhood memories of the sound of barges pounding up the Ohio River as I sat with Gator catching catfish on homemade dough balls. Being on the water always seems to make my thoughts wander back to a time when I had no worries other than what bait to use to catch a fish. Tonight was no exception.

Gator and I never talked much when we were fishing. He always said the fish could hear our voices. It was not until I was much older I realized fish did not have ears. In retrospect, I believe Gator was just teaching me to be comfortable being alone with my thoughts. After he died, I spent many days on the riverbanks by myself, casting a line and munching on beef jerky. I would waste away a soft summer morning while sucking on the sweet stems of honey-suckle flowers. The riverboat captains on the barges would wave as they pushed their payloads down river.

As a kid, I did not understand that Gator was simply preparing me for my life without him. At that age, I believed I would follow Gator to the Everglades. He knew better. He realized that few people could disappear into the Everglades and be happy, least of all, his favorite nephew. He knew my life had been well charted out for me and I was not likely to stray from it. After Gator was gone, the occasional days of silence on the river were my only refuge from life.

I contemplated a lot of youthful decisions from the dry end of a fishing line while sitting on the river bank. What girl to date and what college to attend were decisions that seemed, at the time, to carry with them the weight of the world. After a day of fishing, I could always lie down at night and choose a path that was right for me. As years passed, I gave up my fishing rod for self-help books and after-work happy hours. In retrospect, they never offered me as much clarity as the silence of the river. I should have never traded a Rapalla lure for a three-olive, dirty martini, even if the olives were stuffed with blue cheese.

My thoughts tonight were sharp and as precise as they ever were on the riverbank. The visit with Micco had cleared my head. I was on the path to putting my troubles behind me. That is not to imply that, like some kind of serial killer waiting to snap, I was walking around constantly troubled. I was not. Every day, I left what I thought was a nice home, went to what I felt was a productive job and came home to what I considered was a loving wife. By all outward indicators, my life was good. It was my inner demons haunting me on a daily basis. My failings were based upon what I believed others thought of me rather than what I thought of myself. I lost sight of what was truly valuable in life.

Just as my despair was invisible to all but me, it was also being caused by me. The war for my personal tranquility had been taking place in the small space between my ears. The visit with Micco forced me to understand I was worried about everyone's expectations of me except my own. The problem was I no longer knew what I expected of myself. Was I successful for all I had accomplished? Or was I a failure for never having had the guts to become the person I dreamed of as a kid?

Fishing – time to clear my head.

I found the spot where the guide said I was guaranteed to find fish, cut off the engine and lowered the trolling motor into the water. I set up the fishing seat at the bow of the boat. Once I had tested the foot pedals for the motor, I grabbed my rod-and-reel and tied a spoon lure onto the leader. Lilith remained in her seat, feigning disinterest as she watched.

"How long are we going to stay out here?" Lilith burst out.

My head snapped around. "Shhh," I instructed. "The fish will hear you."

Lilith gave me a funny look, but apparently heeded my odd admonition. She sat back down and again crossed her arms. On about the fifth or sixth cast, I got a bite and yanked hard. The hook set and the fight was on. The reel whizzed as fishing line ran out. I adjusted the drag and pulled back. The rod bent and whipped from side-to-side and I started to crank the fish in.

Lilith stood and walked to the bow. "You got something?"

"Either a fish or a damn big tire," I replied. I nodded my head to the port side compartment. "Grab that net over there," I instructed.

"Why?" Lilith asked.

"Because I need you to scoop the fish out of the water when I get him near the boat." I continued to fight the fish. I had not been salt-water fishing for many years and had forgotten the fight these fish had in them.

"I can't do that," Lilith exclaimed. "I've never done that before."

"Honey, I can't do both," I replied. "Grab the net and dip it in the water when I bring the fish up to the side of the boat." In a somewhat frantic motion, Lilith grabbed the net and kneeled on the bench on the side of the boat. I pulled the fish closer and led it to her. When it was right by her I shouted, "Now." Lilith dipped the net in the water and scooped up the fish. I quickly put down the pole and took the net from Lilith's hand. I pulled the fish out of the net by its gill and held it up. "First one of the night," I said. I looked at Lilith and her mood had clearly changed. She was smiling now and almost as excited as I was.

For the next 45 minutes or so we became a team. I would crank them in and Lilith would scoop them out. I thought about keeping a few to take to Micco, but decided against it. I had no desire to gut fish at this time of night. We released everything we caught. The thrill of the hunt was enough for me for the night.

Lilith was standing behind me when I got a fish on the line and I handed the rod-and-reel to her. Her eyes got big as I stood up and placed her in the fishing chair at the bow of the boat. I got behind her and started whispering instructions in her ear. "Crank easy," I said and then told her to pull back on the rod. It took her awhile, but Lilith finally got the fish to the boat. I netted the fish before lifting it up by a gill. Lilith was laughing. "That was fun," she said. The big grin on her face indicated her sincerity.

She was sitting in the fishing chair as I walked to her holding up her fish. She examined her well-fought trophy and once she was satisfied, Lilith leaned forward and kissed me. "Thanks for bringing me out here," she said.

"I never thought I'd hear you say that tonight," I replied.

"Hard to believe," Lilith said. "But I've actually enjoyed myself."

"That's not so hard to believe," I said, still holding the fish out to my side. "Thanks for coming with me," I said sincerely. I looked deeply into her eyes and we kissed a second time. As I leaned back from our kiss, it was clear to me we were about to be finished with fishing. I walked to the side of the boat and lowered the fish back into the water. It took a minute to reinvigorate him, but when he was ready, he swam off. When I turned around, Lilith had removed her halter and her breasts were naked in the midnight air. She had already unbuckled her shorts and was stepping out of them. When she was completely naked, she sat back down in the chair. "You got what you came out here for," Lilith said softly. "Now it's time for me to get what I want."

Lilith laughed as I moved to cut off the trolling engine, drop the boat's anchor, and rip away at my clothes as quickly as I could. I walked up to the chair and Lilith wrapped her firm legs around me. I slid inside her with ease. Sometimes you need to make love. Other times you just need to fuck. There would be no foreplay tonight. This night, Lilith and I both wanted—no, needed—to just fuck. Sweat poured down our bodies as the moist night air clung to our naked bodies. I was standing as she leaned back in the fishing chair

– her heels on my ass, encouraging my every thrust. No one was near and Lilith was not embarrassed by the primal groans coming from deep in her throat. She dug her fingernails into my arms as her breathing quickened. Lilith was rhythmically growling for me to fuck her harder when she came. I let her recover for a minute and then pounded myself into her and, when I came, it was with similar gusto.

Later, in the quiet of deep night, Lilith sat soundlessly in my lap as I slowly captained the boat back into the channel from where we had started our journey. Neither of us spoke. I wrapped my arm around her waist and my hand softly touched her midriff. That subtle caress was singular and electric. As I moved my hand up and cupped her breast, I kissed her gently on the nape of her neck. The smell of her hair brought back a long-ago memory of my first date – first kiss. For a moment, the touch of Lilith's skin took me back to that alley when I first tasted a kiss and touched bare skin. It reminded me of when such a touch was fresh and the smell of a girl's hair invoked a passion that was new and exciting. I closed my eyes and exhaled as a smile engulfed my face.

The night was perfect.

The ringing of my cell phone woke me from the most sound and peaceful sleep I had encountered in a long time. The phone was by the television and I stumbled over to pick it up. I immediately thought it might be my wife, but the caller identification indicated a Florida-based phone number. It could not be Lilith. She was still asleep in bed.

The only other person in Florida who had my phone number was Catori. A chill ran down my spine and I suddenly did not want to answer the phone. My heart raced as I pushed the accept button.

As Catori spoke, my knees grew weak and my stomach turned over. I stepped carefully back to the bed. Micco was dead.

I had a fleeting thought that I should be crying or doing something other than sitting frozen on the bed as Catori continued to speak. I felt numb.

Lilith pulled herself up and kneeled behind me on the bed. As I hung up the phone, Lilith's arms stole around me and she laid her head on my shoulder. "Oh, baby," she whispered. "I'm so sorry. Was that news about the old man you met up with on the reservation?"

Lilith's touch was comforting, but I sat motionless, continuing to look down at the floor. "That was his son on the phone," I explained. "He died in his sleep about an hour ago."

"That's just horrible," Lilith said.

I sighed heavily. "I'm sorry, Lilith," I said. "But I've got to go up to the reservation."

Lilith drew back a bit. "Right now?" she asked. "In the middle of the night?"

"Yeah," I replied. "I've got to go now."

Lilith started rubbing my shoulders. "You were so relaxed tonight."

"I know." Lilith was right. I had been relaxed.

"So let's go back to bed and you can go up in the morning," Lilith suggested as she continued to rub.

"Let me ask you a question, Lilith," my mind was starting to focus.

"Anything, baby."

"If you could change your course in life," I queried, "would you?"

Lilith chuckled and slapped my arm. "What kind of crazy question is that?" she asked. "You don't have some sort of magic Indian potion, do you?"

Thinking about the proposal Catori had just made to me on the phone caused me to pause. "And what if I did?"

"All this great sex is making you delirious," Lilith replied as she reached down to my crotch.

"Stop," I protested and stood up.

"Okay. Okay," Lilith mumbled. "Man, this is all just a little bit heavy for the middle of the night."

"Just play along with me," I begged.

"All right."

I walked to the window and turned. "If I told you that you could leave with me, right now, and become whatever you always wanted to be, but you had to leave everything else behind," I pondered, "would you do it?"

"If you want me to ride up there with you," Lilith stuttered, "I'd have to be back by noon at the latest."

"No," I replied. "I'm not talking about today. I'm talking about forever. If you could change your life, would you do it?"

Lillith lay back in bed and pulled the sheet around her in a protective manner. She looked past me – out the window. Her eyes looked pained. "No," she mouthed as she shook her head.

"Really?" I asked, amazed at her response. "You've never wanted to change?"

Lilith looked me in the eyes. "That wasn't the question, now was it, sugar?"

"No. You're right, it wasn't."

"Of course, I've wanted to change," Lilith said as she moved to the edge of the bed and looked on the floor for her panties. "Everybody wants to change at some time in their lives. But I'm too far along the path I've chosen. I can't go back."

"Sure you can," I reassured.

"I am who I am," Lilith smiled softly. "Like it or not, I can't or maybe I won't change my path." Lilith finished dressing as she spoke.

I was not surprised by Lilith's answer. I reached down to the floor, pulled on my pants and slipped my feet into my sandals. "I've got to go see Catori," I said. I reached over to the chair and grabbed a t-shirt hanging there.

"Jimmy?" Lilith asked as she approached me.

"What?" I answered as I glanced around the room looking for my wallet and keys.

Lilith stopped in front of me. "You're a good man and I hope you find what you're looking for."

"Thanks," I replied, as my gaze settled back on Lilith. There is a fine line between sexuality and spirituality.

Tears filled Lilith's eyes. "See ya tonight after dinner?" she asked hopefully.

I reached out and wrapped my arms around Lilith drawing her close to me. I kissed her gently. "Sure," I replied. We both knew we would never see each other again.

Chapter Twelve

The full moon shone brightly across the Glades turning the cypress trees almost silver as I pulled onto Alligator Alley. The moonlight reflecting on the water through the intermittent plant life made the entire scene look like a giant jigsaw puzzle, running to the horizon, but only partially complete. All evidence of civilization was hidden by the early morning darkness. I envisioned the Everglades as it must have been experienced by the original Seminoles. The occasional lights of humanity piercing the night were mere distractions to the true beauty of the Everglades. The combination of my surroundings and thoughts of my uncle and Micco, unlocked my frozen emotions and tears. The air was suddenly bitter and humidity choking.

The top was down on my rental car and the wind caused my tears to run into my hair. My gut was clenched tight and my mouth was bone dry. Thoughts were randomly flowing through my head in a million different directions. For all the clarity that had come my way over the past seventy-two hours or so, my mind was currently a muddled mess.

I needed some music and connected my iPhone to the car's audio system. As I drove, I dialed up an early Tom Waits CD. Maybe focusing on the music would make my

pain subside. Like some cruel cosmic mind fuck, Waits went
into one of my favorite songs – *Shiver Me Timbers*.

I'm leavin' my fam'ly,
Leavin' all my friends,
My body's at home,
But my heart's in the wind.
Where the clouds are like headlines,
On a new front page sky,
My tears are salt water
And the moon's full and high.

Ever since I was banging out Dylan tunes on Gator's
Gibson ax on Friday night's at Pete's, music has seemed to
define my life. It has been my refuge and, at times, my ac-
cuser. It seemed damn appropriate I played a song about a
man leaving his family and friends to follow his love of the
sea. In a way, *Shiver Me Timbers* is a glorious account of
the story of my uncle's life and a contemptuous indictment
of my own – the outwardly successful man that failed at his
own dreams and calling.

"Fuck me," I mumbled to myself as I hit my fist repeat-
edly on the steering wheel. I had known Micco for only a
couple of days, yet in a short time, he discovered things
about me I had not known myself. I felt robbed. In many
ways, he led the life I wanted. With Gator at his side, he had
what I should have had by birthright. He had taken my spot.
Hell, maybe I lost a member of my family. I let out a moan
that seemed to emanate from the depths of my soul.

So please call my missus,
Gotta tell her not to cry,
'Cause my goodbye is written,
By the moon in the sky,
Hey and nobody knows me,
I can't fathom my stayin'
Shiver me timbers,
'Cause I'm sailin' away.

I have never been any good at experiencing death. Gator passed on when I was young and I have mourned his loss for a lifetime. The loss of each person following him – my parents, grandparents, friends – seemed to build on a childhood grief from which I never really recovered. The life I wanted for myself died with Gator. When he "crossed over," a piece of me went to the swamp with him, never to cross back. And each death that followed was a grim reminder that I was further and further away from having any chance to recover that part of myself. I wanted to change my path, but I never knew how. Instead, fate became my guide and I was molded into the person I was expected to be.

Angel's death was just as hard on me as Gator's passing. Angel lived much longer than Gator. Like Gator, Angel knew my fate and he tried to make the transition easier for me. Gator had explained my life to me when he gave me the treasured mementos of his life. Angel, on the other hand, spent his life covering for me – knowing that I was outwardly happy, but spiritually unfulfilled. When Angel died, there was a line down the street of people who came to the funeral home to pay their respects. I was so lost that day – my being so empty – I cannot remember but a few who attended.

Since then, I have just been wandering – a rover with a house, but no home. Until my meeting with Micco, I clung to an old guitar and a fishing pole as my only hope of eventual cosmic redemption – occasionally using both of them to capture the peace I so badly sought. In my mind, I understood I was simply fooling myself into tranquility.

Remembering the glorious celebration of Angel's passing made me wonder who would attend my funeral. I laughed out loud as I pondered the small group of people who would cry for my eternal soul.

It is not that I have no true friends. I do. And those who love me will view my casket in solemn mourning. I learned a long time ago that people like me end up having a lot of acquaintances, but much fewer true friends. So I suspect that several of my co-workers will be there battling over my corner office and glass top desk. I know of at least two guys who will show up to check out my widow, Victoria, to see if she looks hot in black. Those from my hometown who had not been blessed with the destiny of success will show up to make sure I really am dead.

I arrived in Florida with a well-constructed foundation of personal melancholy. Micco and Catori changed my attitude. With them at my personal helm, I suddenly felt alive again. I could not recover my past, but they had provided me a near-blood connection. We had played music together – fished together – and shared black tea. We shared the memory of my uncle. One day Micco and Catori were unknown to me. The next day they were my blood – Micco my brother and Catori my son. That missing part of my life seemed as close as the end of the Everglades horizon in front of me. But just like you can never make it to the horizon …

Micco was gone and I was faced with a choice.

I reflected back to the plane flight on my birthday – the one that brought me to Florida and started this entire bizarre adventure. I thought about the young people I saw on the plane. As I drove in the shadows of the Glades, it dawned on me. I had failed to appreciate the happiness of the young parents laughing and smiling on the plane. They were smiling for the sheer delight of the moment. They were living for that singular place in time. They felt no remorse for the past and no fear of the future. Their ability to find piece of mind in such a simplistic form was something that has often been lost on previous generations.

My old man's generation worked in the same place most of their lives and got a gold watch and a fixed pension as a reward for their success. When our parents retired, their kids, us, saw them as too old and too poor to enjoy their golden years. The Greatest Generation was old and underappreciated.

So my generation revised the definition of success. We decided that to attain success we needed to get more money quicker and retire younger. We jumped around from job to job for incremental salary changes, but we put little of it away for later in life. When we started looking at retirement, we discovered that we had nice wide-screen televisions, but little cash to go find the later-in-life happiness that escaped our parents. We lay in bed at night praying for a peaceful death to escape what had become the burden of our lives, awaking in a cold sweat to find ourselves in yet another day.

Today's generation is trying to learn from the mistakes of two generations and working to find success in the form of instant enjoyment. I used to chide people at my company who were clock-watchers – employees who refused to work a minute longer than quitting time. These kids chide their colleagues who do not watch the clock. They want to be away from work searching for what excites them at that very moment.

This generation has figured out earlier than us that corporations have no loyalty – people do. They do not live for their work and retirement. They live for their present.

And so did my Uncle Gator. He discovered his true path back in the 50s. For following his dream, he was an outcast to some and a Renaissance man to others. In truth, he was a Gen-Xer long before his time.

All my life, I wanted to be like Gator. I wanted to be the freewheeling man-of-all-seasons. Then, as I grew up, I hopped so many different corporate trains that I became an institutional hobo, riding the company rails while searching for meaning in life. I followed the path in life that was pre-destined for me by others, so that I could hopefully – finally – follow my dream, that is, if I was not too old to carry it out.

Today I will finally change it all. I will right the path and figure out where that zag may have taken me that day when I zigged instead.

Many people curse Florida because of its seemingly un-changing climate. Blue skies, hot and humid can wear on some people. It is for that precise reason I love Florida weather – particularly in the Glades. The sun was not any-where near in the sky, yet the air was thick and wet. A musty smell permeated my nose. A chorus of crickets, frogs, and owls sang along with the tunes playing on my iPhone.

I pulled off onto the side road to the bar where I first met Micco and saw the red taillights of the old orange pickup truck in the parking lot. I pulled in beside the truck and got out of the car. Catori was sitting in the driver's seat. Onida was sitting next to him staring out the passenger window.

Her hair was tussled and missing the decorative peyote beads in her braids, the response to death for a traditional Seminole squaw. I looked in the bed of the truck. An old Indian blanket covered the body of Micco.

"I'm sorry," I said to Catori and Onida as I approached the driver's window. It sounded shallow, but I did not quite know what else to say. "I really am."

"I know you are," Catori replied as he shut off the engine. He got out of the truck and I hugged him. Onida approached from around the back of the truck. She and I hugged. The embrace was long as if I hoped to pull Onida's agony from her. Finally, she pushed back. Tears were running down her cheeks and her voice was soft, barely audible. "Micco had just met you, but he felt a shared kinship with you." She reached up and tossed back some hair that had fallen in her face. "He didn't trust many white men, but he trusted you."

"I'm glad," I replied as I looked at her round, moon face. I forced a smile. "My life is better for having known him. He completed something in me."

"And you in him," Onida replied, nodding.

I walked to the back of the pickup and lifted the blanket off Micco's body. His face had a tranquil look to it. The deep, wrinkled lines caused by years of worry for the fate of his tribe had softened. I closed my eyes and touched his forehead as if to somehow transmit his peace to me. My own breathing steadied as I silently said a prayer for Micco's soul.

I nearly forgot that Onida was with us until she made a gentle cough, clearly done to let me know that it was she and her son's turn. I moved away and Onida gently stroked Micco's long grey hair. Catori placed his hand on his mom's shoulder.

I did not want to interrupt the intimacy of the scene, so I waited a few moments before I spoke. "You sure you want to do this?" I asked softly. "You could get in trouble, you know."

Onida turned to me and held her chin up high. "Your government may have jurisdiction over you, but it has none over me." Onida turned for a final look at Micco. As she placed the blanket back over Micco, she spoke with confidence in her voice. "My soul is only governed by the Master of Breath." Once she had tucked the blanket around Micco's body, she looked at me.

Catori spoke for them both. "And you?" Onida's stare had a chilling insight to it. I looked at her as Catori continued to speak. "Are you ready? There is no going back from what we have discussed."

"I understand." Catori did not have to point it out to me. The enormity of my decision had been on my mind ever since I had received his phone call. Its finality was overwhelming. "I am as ready as any man that has been given only a few hours to change the course of his life."

"And he has searched a lifetime for inner-peace," Onida interjected. "I think what we are about to do will bring it to him."

I was looking for the right words to say. What we had discussed was unconscionable to most people. But I had made my choice. Time was my enemy, only allowing cowardice and retreat. It was time for me to finally take control of my own destiny. "My uncle once told me that it is up to the wife of a Seminole man to choose the final resting place of her husband," I said.

"Yes," Onida said, "that is our tradition." She looked at me and knew I was ready. "And, you should know that I choose this freely, as well."

I looked at Onida as she spent her last private moments with her husband. I walked to the front of the pickup to give her a few minutes to herself. I started to light up a cigarette when something startled me. I stopped and froze. Another set of car lights approached up the gravel road followed by a cloud of dust.

"Don't worry," Catori said as the car pulled in beside mine. "It's only Dr. Yanah. After I spoke to you, I called him and told him to meet us here."

I watched as Dr. Yanah got out of his Mercedes. He was a middle-aged, pudgy man with a dark receding hairline. I remembered his name as the tribal doctor from the article that Everton Santiago has shown me on my first day at the resort.

Dr. Yanah walked up to the truck and hugged Onida. He looked in the bed of the truck and then at me. "Micco was a good man," he said as if implying that I would have a hard time living up to his legacy.

"I know," I replied. Yanah stared at me as if hoping to see doubt. I squared up my shoulders and jaw as my eyes never wavered. He nodded at me in apparent approval. Together he, Catori and I grabbed Micco's body from the bed of the pickup truck. We unrolled him from the blanket and put him in the front seat of my rental car.

While we were adjusting Micco's body behind the driver's wheel, Catori grabbed a can of gasoline from the back of the truck. We stepped back as Catori doused gasoline over the interior of the car and Micco's body. Onida approached the car, leaned in, whispered something in Micco's ear and then gently kissed him on the forehead.

As Onida reached into her pocket for matches, I suddenly stopped her. "Hang on," I said. "Shit, I nearly forgot." I reached inside the car and popped open the trunk of the car. I ran to the back and grabbed Gator's old fishing pole and Gibson guitar from the trunk. I walked over and placed both gently in the cab of the truck.

Onida was whispering a prayer. I was not sure if the prayer was Christian or Seminole and even less sure that it mattered. I wondered if she and I had prayed to the same Maker. My heart was beating rapidly, but not with anxiety. I was about to be a free man. In a few minutes, I would become the man I had dreamed of being my entire life. I was staring fate in the eye and fate was blinking.

Onida lit a match and tossed it inside the car.

As the flames quickly spread, Dr. Yanah looked at me. "Give me your wallet," he instructed. I did and he tossed it onto the ground beside the burning car.

The heat from the fire reached our faces, so we stepped back a bit. We watched as the flames engulfed the car. "So what happens now?" I asked.

"Now," Yanah said without making eye contact, "I get called out to investigate a fire on the reservation. I find the wallet of a white tourist gone fishing in the Glades and declare it's your corpse in the car. We cremate the body and send your ashes with my report to the authorities." Flames were jumping wildly into the night air. "We need to be going now," he said without emotion.

Tears filled my eyes as I watched myself die and be reborn in Micco's funeral pyre. I pulled out my smart phone, engaged Facebook and posted a status update. "Headed to the Everglades to fish." I hit the send button, leaned back and then heaved my cell phone as far as I could into the crystal clear water of the Florida Everglades. A deep sense of euphoria came over me. I did it. I was free.

Catori cocked his head. "What did you do that for?" he asked quizzically.

I thought of Gator and smiled. "I want to make sure that none of my belongings will keep me from crossing over."

"Crossing over?" Onida asked. "Over what?"

"Whatever's next," I said as I got into the pickup truck and cranked the starter. "Whatever's next."

Acknowledgements

Everybody has one book in them and I spent thirty years writing the wrong one.

In 1975, Jack Graham and I had the distinct pleasure of spending the day with Kentucky's greatest writer, Jesse Stuart. From that day forward, for thirty years, I tried to follow Stuart's path by writing the great coming-of-age novel. The fact that, for three decades, I failed to get past the third chapter would indicate to most that I had never come of age. I finally got to Chapter Four because of my son, Zachary, who challenged me to write *Alligator Alley* during National Novel Writing Month. It took a little longer to write than the suggested 30 days sought by NaNoWriMo, but without Zach's challenge to me, this book would today still be an unfulfilled dream. Thank you, son. The drive to write this book is the greatest present you could have ever given to me.

Though I changed his name in the book, Gator, was based on my great uncle, Chip Thompson, a real person. Whether he was loved or loathed depends on which side of the family you're on. Bill Gaither fished with him on a regular basis and told me stories that made their way into this book as my own. With the minor exception of a few name changes, the newspaper articles about the alligators in Devou Park are also real and were discovered in an old family scrapbook by my cousin, Terry Bethel.

Many of Jimmy's flashbacks are tales told to me by people I grew up with in Ludlow: Steve Bodkin, Jack Glueck, Pat Crowley, and Bob Schrage. I'll leave it to them to defend the truthfulness of their stories. Thanks to Paul Alley for introducing me to the Ocean Reef Club in Key Largo and to Everton Darling for mixing the finest rum drink in the Keys.

When I am finishing up a book, I tend to go to odd places to write. When I pony up to the bar at Indigo's, Mike Hang keeps my laptop plugged in and my glass full of Guinness. People who frequent Joseph-Beth in Crestview Hills must think I'm an employee. I'm there enough to be eligible for benefits. The manager there, Craig Sherman, offered a lot of good comments as I finished this novel.

At the young age of four, Jim "Scorch" Chastain was thrown from an airboat and raised by wild boars in the Everglades. He gave me insight I could have never gotten from a research trip to the library. This book is his. Thanks to Bobby McCabe and Chief Wade DeHate for keeping me out of trouble when we went to the Glades with Scorch.

As this novel is a deviation from my normal genre, I was very nervous about showing it to my sample readers. Thanks to Robin DeHate, Jim and Kathy Brewer, Debbie Streitelmeier, Teri Stewart, Paul Alley, Sis Deiters, Don Lemrhul, Karen Renz, Aref Bsisu, Ginny Shephard, Eric Haas, Dennis Hetzel and John Carey for giving me the courage to press forward. I should publish the notes that Mark Morris sends me when he reviews my manuscripts. They would be best sellers.

My editor, Jeff Landen, understood, encouraged and helped me clarify the personal angst of Jimmy. In drives from book show to book show, my publicist, Debbie McKinney, put up with the rants and ramblings that became the pages of this book. Kevin Kelly did more for me than just create another great cover. He kept me going when I wanted to quit.

With four political thrillers in print, it was a giant leap of faith for my publisher to allow me a literary novel. Thanks to Cathy Teets and the folks at Headline Books for having faith in me and letting me finish a project three decades in the making.

Zach may have inspired me to write this book, but it's written for him, his brother, Josh, and his sister, MacKenzie. Someday I hope you'll come to understand the message of Alligator Alley.

To my wife Linda – editor, lover, and best friend – I love you today more than ever.

Other Books by Rick Robinson

Novels
Writ of Mandamus
The Maximum Contribution
Sniper Bid
Manifest Destiny

Non-Fiction
Strange Bedfellow

About the Author

Rick's previous novel, *Writ of Mandamus* was named Grand Prize Winner at the London Book Festival January 2012 and Rick Robinson carried off honors as International Independent Author of the Year. It was named Best Fiction at the Indie Book Awards.

Best selling author P.J. O'Rourke says that Rick Robinson "may be the only person on Earth who both understands the civics book chapter on 'How a Bill Becomes a Law' and knows how to get good seats at the Kentucky Derby."

Robinson's third novel, *Manifest Destiny*, was named 2010 Independent Book of the Year and he was awarded 2010 Independent Author of the Year. *Manifest Destiny* was also a Winner at the Paris and New York Book Festivals along with Finalist Awards in the USA News Best Book Awards for Best Thriller/Adventure, Best Fiction Indie Book Awards, Best Thriller Indie Excellence Book Awards, Best Thriller International Book Awards, and Honorable Mentions at the San Francisco, Hollywood, London, and Beach Book Festivals. This title has also been optioned by film producer, Peter Dyell, and is headed for the big screen in the future.

Rick's first book, *The Maximum Contribution*, and his second novel, *Sniper Bid*, both won major book awards.

Rick Robinson has thirty years experience in politics and law, including a stint on Capitol Hill as Legislative Director/Chief Counsel to then-Congressman Jim Bunning (R-KY). He has been active in all levels of politics, from advising candidates on the national level to walking door-to-door in city council races. He ran for the United States Congress in 1998.